MY JACQUELINE WILSON TREASURY

www.randomhousechildrens.co.uk

MY JACQUELINE WILSON TREASURY

Illustrated by Nick Sharratt

DOUBLEDAY

MY JACQUELINE WILSON TREASURY
A DOUBLEDAY BOOK 978 0 857 53422 4

SLEEPOVERS
First published in Great Britain by Doubleday,
an imprint of Random House Children's Publishers UK
A Random House Group Company
Text © Jacqueline Wilson, 2001
Illustrations © Nick Sharratt, 2001

TRACY BEAKER'S THUMPING HEART
First published in Great Britain by Corgi Yearling,
an imprint of Random House Children's Publishers UK
A Random House Group Company
Text © Jacqueline Wilson, 2009
Illustrations © Nick Sharratt, 2009

THE MUM-MINDER
First published in Great Britain by Doubleday,
an imprint of Random House Children's Publishers UK
A Random House Group Company
Text © Jacqueline Wilson, 1993
Illustrations © Nick Sharratt, 1993

THE CAT MUMMY
First published in Great Britain by Doubleday,
an imprint of Random House Children's Publishers UK
A Random House Group Company
Text © Jacqueline Wilson, 2001
Illustrations © Nick Sharratt, 2001

ODD ONE OUT
First published in Great Britain in *Eating Candyfloss Upside Down* by Puffin,
Reprinted in *Totally Jacqueline Wilson* by Doubleday,
an imprint of Random House Children's Publishers UK
A Random House Group Company
Text © Jacqueline Wilson, 2003
Illustrations © Nick Sharratt, 2003

LIZZIE ZIPMOUTH
First published in Great Britain by Young Corgi,
an imprint of Random House Children's Publishers UK
A Random House Group Company
Text © Jacqueline Wilson, 2000
Illustrations © Nick Sharratt, 2000

This collection first published in Great Britain as MY JACQUELINE WILSON TREASURY
by Doubleday, an imprint of Random House Children's Publishers UK
A Random House Group Company

This edition published 2014

1 3 5 7 9 10 8 6 4 2

Text copyright © Jacqueline Wilson, 2014
Illustrations copyright © Nick Sharratt, 2014

The right of Jacqueline Wilson to be identified as the author of this work has been
asserted in accordance with the Copyright, Designs and Patents Act 1988.

The Random House Group Limited supports the Forest Stewardship Council (FSC®), the leading international forest
certification organization. Our books carrying the FSC label are printed on FSC®-certified paper. FSC is the only
forest certification scheme supported by the leading environmental organizations, including Greenpeace.
Our paper procurement policy can be found at www.randomhouse.co.uk/environment.

Set in Blueprint and New Century Schoolbook LT

Doubleday Books are published by Random House Children's Publishers UK,
61–63 Uxbridge Road, London W5 5SA

www.**randomhousechildrens**.co.uk
www.**totallyrandombooks**.co.uk
www.**randomhouse**.co.uk

Addresses for companies within The Random House Group Limited can be found at:
www.**randomhouse**.co.uk/offices.htm

THE RANDOM HOUSE GROUP Limited Reg. No. 954009

A CIP catalogue record for this book is available from the British Library.

Printed in China

☆ CONTENTS ☆

SLEEPOVERS

For Kate
With many thanks

☆ CHAPTER ONE ☆

'Guess what!' said Amy. 'It's my birthday next week and my mum says I can invite all my special friends for a sleepover party.'

'Great,' said Bella.

'Fantastic,' said Chloe.

'Wonderful,' said Emily.

I didn't say anything. I just smiled. Hopefully.

I wasn't sure if I was one of Amy's *special* friends. Amy and Bella were best friends. Chloe and Emily were best friends. I didn't have a best friend yet at this new school.

Well, it wasn't quite a new school, it was quite old, with winding stairs and long polished corridors and lots and lots of classrooms, some of them in Portakabins in the playground. I still got a bit lost sometimes. The very first day I couldn't find the girls' toilets and went hopping round all playtime, getting desperate. But then Emily found me and took me to the toilets herself. I liked Emily *sooooo* much. I wished she could be my best friend. But she already had Chloe for her best friend.

I didn't think much of Chloe.

I liked Amy and Bella though. We'd started to go round in a little bunch of five, Amy and Bella and Emily and Chloe and me. We formed this special secret club. We called ourselves the Alphabet Girls. It's because of our names. I'm Daisy. So our first names start with A B C D and E. I was the one who spotted this. The secret club was all my idea too.

I always wanted to be part of a special secret club. It was almost as good as having a best friend.

I wasn't sure if Amy's birthday sleepover was strictly reserved for best friends only. Amy went on talking and talking about her sleepover and how she knew she wasn't going to sleep all night long. Bella teased her because one time when Amy spent the night at Bella's she fell sound asleep at nine o'clock and didn't wake up till nine o'clock the next morning. Chloe said she sometimes didn't go to bed till ever so late, eleven or even twelve at night, so she'd stay awake, no bother. Emily said she always woke up early now because her new baby brother started crying for his bottle at six o'clock every single day.

I still didn't say anything. I tried to keep on smiling.

Emily looked at me. Then she looked at Amy.

'Hey, Amy. Daisy can come too, can't she?'

'Of course,' said Amy.

My mouth smiled until it almost tickled my ears.

'Whoopee!' I yelled.

'Really, Daisy!' said Chloe, clutching her ears in an affected way. 'You practically deafened me.'

'Sorry,' I said – though I wasn't. But you have to try to keep on the right side of Chloe. She's the one who tells everyone what to do. The Boss.

She even tried to tell Amy what to do at her own sleepover. 'You've got to get some seriously scary videos, right?' she said.

'My mum won't let me watch *seriously* scary videos,' said Amy.

'Don't tell your mum. Just wait till she's gone to bed and then we can all watch in your bedroom,' said Chloe, sighing because she thought it was so simple.

'I don't have a video recorder in my bedroom, just a portable television,' said Amy.

'I haven't even got my own television,' said Bella comfortingly. 'Never mind. Hey, what are you going to have for your birthday tea, Amy?'

Bella likes food. She always has big bars of chocolate at break-time. She eats eight squares herself. She gives Amy three squares because she's her best friend, but she lets Chloe and Emily and me have one square each. Chloe sometimes gobbles the last square too. Chloe gets away with murder.

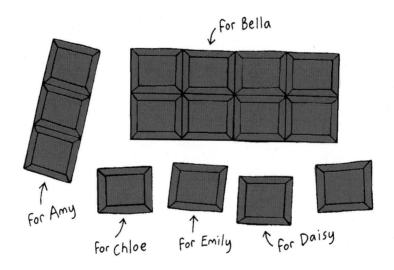

'Mum says I can have a big birthday cake,' said Amy. She smiled at Bella. '*Chocolate* cake!'

'No, have an iced cake in a special shape. They're seriously cool,' said Chloe.

'Amy can have what she likes. It's her sleepover,' said Bella.

Chloe frowned.

'We can *all* have sleepovers on our birthdays,' said Emily quickly.

'Then we can each choose the way we want them to be. If we're allowed. My mum's going nuts looking after my baby brother but I *think* she'll let me have a sleepover.'

'Mine will too,' said Bella.

'My mum lets me do anything I like,' said Chloe. 'So does my dad.'

I didn't say anything. I hoped they wouldn't notice. But they were all looking at me.

'Can you have a sleepover too, Daisy?' said Emily.

'Oh sure,' I said quickly, but my heart started thumping under my new school sweatshirt.

It wasn't my birthday *yet*, thank goodness.

I couldn't have a sleepover party. I didn't want to tell them why. I might have told Emily by herself. But I didn't want to tell the others. Especially not Chloe.

☆ CHAPTER TWO ☆

I told Mum about Amy's sleepover party while we were having tea.
'That's lovely, Daisy,' she said, but I could tell she wasn't really
listening. She was too busy concentrating on feeding my sister, Lily.

'There now, Lily, yum yum,' Mum mumbled,
spooning yoghurt into Lily's mouth.
Mum's own mouth opened and
shut. Lily's mouth didn't always
open and shut at the right time.
It snapped shut so the spoon
clanked against her teeth, or
suddenly gaped open so the yoghurt drooled down her chin.

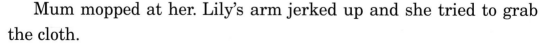

Mum mopped at her. Lily's arm jerked up and she tried to grab
the cloth.

'There! Did you see that, Daisy? Lily's trying to wipe her own chin.
Clever girl, Lily!'

'Mm, clever girl,' I said.

My sister Lily isn't clever. She isn't my little baby sister. She isn't little at all. She's my big sister. She's eleven years old but she isn't in the top year at school. Lily doesn't go to my new school. She didn't go to my old school either. She never used to go to school at all, she just stayed at home with Mum, but now she goes to this new special school. That's why we moved, so that she could go there. It's a special school because Lily has special needs. That's the right way to describe her. There are lots and lots of *wrong* ways. Some children at my old school used to call Lily horrible names when they saw Mum pushing her in the street. They used to call me names too.

I don't think Emily would call Lily horrible names. Or Amy or Bella. But I'm not at all sure about Chloe.

I'd shut up about my sister Lily since I'd started to go to this new school. I didn't want anyone calling her names.

Though *I* call her names sometimes. I get mad at her. She isn't like a real sister. We can't play together and swap clothes and dance and giggle and mess about. She's not like a big sister because she can't ever tell me stuff and hold my hand across roads and watch out for me at school. She's not like a little sister either because she's too big to sit on my lap and she's too heavy for me to carry around. It's even getting a struggle to push her in her wheelchair.

Something went wrong with Lily when she was born. She won't ever be able to walk or talk. Well, that's what Dad says. Mum says we just don't know. Dad says we do know, but Mum won't face facts. Mum and Dad have rows about Lily and I hate it. Sometimes I almost hate her because she's always in the way and she cries a lot and she wakes us all up in the night and she takes up so much time. But I always feel lousy if I'm mean to Lily. I get into her bed at night when Mum and Dad are asleep and I whisper sorry in Lily's ear. I cuddle her. She doesn't exactly cuddle me back but she acts like she's glad I'm there. She makes these little soft sounds. I pretend it's Lily talking to me in her own secret language. I whisper secrets to her under the covers and she whispers, 'Ur ur ur ur ur' back to me. It's as if we're having our own tiny private sleepover just for us.

I got into bed with her that night and told her all about Amy's sleepover. I've told her all about Amy and Bella. I've told her heaps about Emily and how I wish she could be my best friend. I've told her heaps about Chloe too and how I wish she didn't sometimes act like she was my worst enemy.

'What's that you're saying, Lily?' I whispered. 'Oh, I get it! You say that Emily's probably going to get seriously fed up with Chloe being so mean and moody all the time. You think she's going to break friends with her and be *my* best friend instead?'

Lily went, 'Ur ur ur ur ur.'

I gave her a grateful hug. Sometimes I was almost glad she was my sister.

☆ CHAPTER THREE ☆

Amy and Bella and Chloe and Emily and I all got very excited about the sleepover party. We talked about it all the time at school. We talked about it so much that our teacher Mrs Graham got cross with us.

She got especially cross with Chloe because her voice was the loudest. She kept her in at playtime. I had a lovely playtime with Emily. She said she liked my long hair and wished she could brush it, so I undid my plaits and then we played hairdressers and I was a posh lady going to a dance and Emily was fixing my hair for me, and she gave me a facial too, with soap from the washbasins in the girls' cloakrooms. I didn't wash all the soap off properly so my face felt a bit stiff when we went into the classroom. It went stiffer still when I saw Chloe glaring at me. I knew she was going to get me.

'You mean pig, Daisy!' she yelled as soon as it was going-home time. 'It was all *your* fault. *You* were saying something stupid about how you've never been to a sleepover before so I said you can't have had any friends at your old school and then Mrs Graham got cross with me when I didn't start saying stuff, it was *you*. Why didn't you tell her it was all your fault?'

'It wasn't really Daisy's *fault*,' said Emily.

'Yes it was! She wouldn't own up. She let me take the blame. She's horrible. I don't know why we have to have her tagging around with us all the time,' said Chloe.

'Don't be like that, Chloe,' said Emily, putting her arm round her. 'Here, do you want a chocolate biscuit? I saved it for you.'

Chloe wouldn't take the chocolate biscuit so Bella ate it.

'Are you really having a chocolate cake for your birthday, Amy?' said Bella.

'Yeah, my mum's friend's making it. And we're having egg sandwiches and sausages on sticks and cheese and pineapple and fancy ice-creams and special fruity drinks with teeny umbrellas,' said Amy, her eyes shining.

'Like grown-up cocktails,' I said.

'Is Daisy still coming to your sleep-over?' said Chloe.

My heart started thumping.

But Emily was quick.

'Course she is. We're all coming. Hey, I can't wait till it's my sleepover party. If my mum lets me have one.'

'*My* mum will let me. She lets me do *anything*. I'm going to have the best sleepover party ever, you'll see,' said Chloe.

I was pretty sure I wasn't going to be invited to Chloe's sleepover party. I didn't care. But I did desperately want to go to Amy's.

'Of course you can still come, Daisy,' Amy whispered in my ear.

I gave Amy a quick hug. I decided I liked Amy almost as much as Emily.

I went shopping with Mum to buy Amy a birthday present. I thought I might buy her a grown-up fountain pen as she liked writing. I wanted to spend a long time choosing, but Lily was with us too, of course, and she was having a bad day, crying a lot.

People started staring at us and it made Lily more upset. She cried and cried very loudly.

'*Do* hurry up and choose Amy's present!' said Mum.

I couldn't decide which colour fountain pen Amy would like best. Bright red? Lime green? Sunny yellow? Sky blue? Amy liked wearing all different bright colours. I didn't know which was her favourite.

'Daisy! We'll have to go,' Mum said.

Lily was bright red in the face herself – and screaming.

I suddenly saw a plastic case of special metallic roller pens all different colours: pink and orange and emerald and purple and turquoise, even gold and silver. I thought how great it would look writing with all these different colours.

'Can I get these for Amy, Mum? Please?'

They were more expensive than the fountain pens but Mum was so keen to get us out of Smith's that she didn't argue.

I hoped Amy would like her special coloured pens. *I'd* have liked a great big set like that. I'd had a lovely purple metallic pen but Lily had got hold of it and spoilt the tip so that it could only write in splotches.

I would have loved to try Amy's pens (just to make sure they worked all right) but as soon as we got home and Mum got Lily changed and fed and calmed down she wrapped Amy's pen set in a piece of pink tissue paper and tied it with my old crimson hair ribbon.

Amy's present looked beautiful. I wished *I* looked beautiful on Saturday afternoon when I was ready to go to the party. Emily had promised me she wouldn't be wearing a proper party dress, just her favourite trousers and T-shirt, so I hadn't worn my dress either. I had serious doubts about my dress anyway. It had embroidered teddy bears all across the chest. I'd liked them at first but now I felt sure Chloe would say I looked babyish. I had teddies on my pyjamas too, but I hoped that wouldn't matter. They were very old pyjamas and getting a bit small but they were my favourites. I also had my *own* teddy. He's very little and a deep shade of navy blue. I call him Midnight. I can't get to sleep without him, but he's so small I hoped to hide him in my hand so Chloe couldn't tease me.

Dad drove me over to Amy's house. I was very, very, very glad I didn't have to walk there with Mum and Lily.

'You have a lovely time, Daisy,' said Dad, when we got there.

I didn't say anything.

I hoped and hoped and hoped I *would* have a lovely time.

☆ CHAPTER FOUR ☆

I was very glad I hadn't worn my teddy dress. Everyone was wearing tops and trousers. Emily said she specially liked my top with the silver starry pattern. I twinkled just like stars.

Amy liked her metallic pens a lot.

'Wow! I *love* these pens. Now I've got one of every single colour. Let's try them out, eh?'

'We don't want to do writing at a party,' said Chloe. 'Let's play some music and dance.'

So we all trooped into Amy's living room. It had big red velvet sofas and fluffy white rugs and lots and lots of china ornaments. We can't have velvet and furry things at home because Lily makes too much mess, and she waves her arms about too much for any china ornaments to be safe. *We* waved our arms around wildly while we were dancing but Amy's mum didn't fuss at all, and she let us have the music up ever so loud.

Amy's two big sisters showed us how to do this brilliant dance.

Bella kept turning the wrong way and mixing up her left and right but Alison and Abigail were very patient. I got a *bit* mixed up myself at first but I caught on quite quickly. Quicker than Chloe, actually. Amy knew the dance already so she was very good at it – but not as good as Emily. Emily is magic at dancing.

We did this special dance over and over until we all knew it backwards (though Bella still faced backwards if you didn't watch her). Then we performed it like a real girl group to Amy's mum and her dad and her nan and they all clapped and clapped and said we were great.

Then we had our tea and there was the chocolate cake Amy had promised. It was chocolate sponge inside with three layers of chocolate cream and there were even little chocolate drops all round the frosted chocolate icing on the top of the cake. I had a big slice and it tasted wonderful at first but I couldn't actually finish it. Bella finished it for me. She had her own slice *and* a second helping. Bella is astonishing.

When we were all full – even Bella – we watched cartoons on television for a bit, and then we went upstairs with Alison and Abigail and they let us dress up in their special glittery clubbing clothes and stagger round in their high heels. We looked *wonderful*. Almost grown up!

Amy is so lucky having big sisters like Alison and Abigail. Abigail is only three years older than Lily. I imagined what it would be like if Lily's brain hadn't been damaged and she could dress me up in cool clothes and teach me dances.

I felt a little bit sad but then we watched some more funny shows on television – Amy can get ever so many different channels – and I cheered up. I felt especially pleased that when we all sat together on the beautiful red velvet sofa I was in the middle, with Amy one side and Emily the other.

I didn't get so lucky when we all went up to Amy's bedroom to sort out who was sleeping where. Amy has bunk beds so Bella got to go on the top bunk above Amy. Amy's mum had made up a mattress on most of Amy's floor for two more girls.

'That's fine for Emily and me,' said Chloe.

'It's a very big mattress,' said Emily. 'I'm sure there's heaps of room for Daisy too.'

'No, it would be much too much of a squash,' said Chloe firmly. 'Daisy had better have that camp bed thing in the corner.'

So I had to make do with the camp bed. It didn't really matter at first because we didn't get *into* bed for hours after we got into our pyjamas. We all played trampolines on the mattress and sang along to tapes on Amy's cassette recorder and painted our nails all different colours with Alison and Abigail's old nail varnishes.

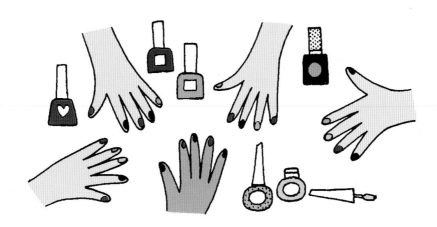

Amy's mum put her head round the door at ten o'clock and said she thought we should start settling down. We didn't settle down for ages and ages. After we'd all gone to the bathroom together and cleaned our teeth (and squirted each other with Amy's dad's shaving foam) Bella said she felt peckish. Amy ran down to the kitchen and came back with a big bag of crisps and the remains of the birthday cake.

We nibbled crisps and ate baby slices of cake as if we were sitting up properly at the tea table, but then we started messing around, scraping icing off the top of the cake with our fingers and seeing how many crisps we could put in our mouths all at once. Bella made herself a chocolate cake crisp sandwich. She said it tasted totally delicious. She wanted us all to try a bite but I decided not to. Emily had a big bite to please Bella – and then went very, very quiet.

'What's up with you, Emily?' said Chloe. 'You're not sleepy already, are you?'

'No. I just feel a bit sick,' said Emily in a tiny voice.

'Yuck! I'm not sure I want to share the mattress with you now. You're not to be sick on me,' said Chloe.

'I won't actually *be* sick,' said Emily, but she didn't sound too sure.

Amy's mum said we really had to get into bed now. She looked a little fussed about the crisp crumbs and chocolate smears but she couldn't get really cross on Amy's birthday. She made us all go and clean our teeth again and do a last wee, and then we all got into our different beds and she said good night and switched off the light.

We didn't go to sleep of course. Amy and Bella and Chloe and I talked and talked. Emily didn't say anything.

'Are you asleep, Emily?' I asked.

'No,' said Emily.

'You're not still feeling sick, are you?' said Chloe.

'No,' said Emily – but after a minute she got out of bed and ran to the bathroom.

'Yuck yuck yuck! She *is* going to be sick,' said Chloe.

'Maybe I should call my mum,' said Amy.

'I'll go and see if she's all right,' I said.

I went to help Emily. When she'd finished being sick I mopped her up and gave her a drink of water and put my arm round her. She was shivering.

'You're so kind, Daisy,' she whispered, hugging me back. 'I wish you were my best friend.'

'I wish I was too.'

We both sighed. Then we went back to Amy's room and Emily got into bed with Chloe.

I very quietly fished in my bag and found Midnight. He came underneath the covers with me and we cuddled up in the lonely little camp bed.

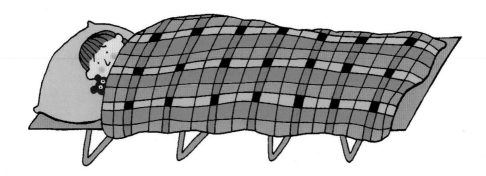

☆ CHAPTER FIVE ☆

It was Bella's birthday next. 'I'm going to have a sleepover party too,' she said.

'Who's coming?' said Chloe.

I worried.

'We're *all* coming, silly!' said Bella. 'It's going to be great. I'm going to have a h-u-g-e cake.'

'Is it going to be a chocolate cake?' Emily asked weakly.

'No, it's not. It's going to be a big *blue* cake, and you don't get blue chocolate.'

'I didn't think you got blue *cakes*,' said Chloe.

'Ah! This is a special one, because my party's going to be extra specially-special,' said Bella. 'We're all going swimming. My birthday cake's going to have blue icing because it's in the shape of a swimming pool.'

We all agreed this *was* specially-special. Even Chloe seemed impressed. 'I'm brilliant at swimming. Great idea! Though wait till you hear what I'm doing for my sleepover party,' she said.

'What?'

'*Aha!*' she said.

'I still don't know if I can *have* a sleepover party,' said Emily. 'I keep asking my mum and she says there's no point anyone coming to my house because you can't get any sleep as my baby brother cries all night. I *hope* she's just joking. Though she doesn't make many jokes now. She's too tired.'

'Never mind, Emily. We don't all have to have sleepover parties,' I said quickly. 'I'm not sure *my* mum will let me.'

'Why? You haven't got a baby brother too, have you?' said Chloe, frowning at me.

'No. I've got a sister, but . . .'

'But what?'

I shrugged, my heart thumping. 'Oh. You know,' I said – though of course they *didn't* know.

I started madly hoping that Lily might start to get a lot better so that it wouldn't be so bad. Mum said Lily was improving in leaps and bounds now she was at her new special school. Lily couldn't *really* leap or bound. She couldn't walk. She couldn't even crawl.

'But she's on the way to becoming more mobile,' said Mum. 'She loves her swimming, don't you, Lily? You bob along like a little duck.'

Lily's special school had its own small swimming pool. Lily couldn't really swim. They just held her in the water while she splashed a bit.

'*I* can swim ever so fast now, Mum,' I said. 'Hey, did I tell you, Bella's having a special swimming party?'

'You told me lots of times, Daisy,' said Mum.

'I do sometimes have to put my foot on the bottom though,' I said. 'I think Bella and Amy and Emily and Chloe might be able to swim a bit better than me. Especially Chloe.'

'Shall I take you swimming on Sunday morning?' said Dad. 'Then you can have a little practice swim.'

'That's a lovely idea,' said Mum. She looked at Lily. I worried that *they* might want to come too.

'Yes, let's, Dad,' I said quickly. 'Just you and me.'

Lily couldn't understand but I felt a bit mean even so. I got into her bed that night and snuggled up to her.

'Do you really like swimming, Lily?' I asked. Lily went, 'Ur ur ur,' as if she really did. 'Well, when I get a bit bigger *I'll* take you swimming,' I said.

Lily went, 'Ur ur ur ur ur,' as if she'd like that very much.

I went swimming with Dad on Sunday and we had a great time. Dad showed me how to kick out with my legs like a little frog and I swam ever such a long way without putting my foot down once. Then we played jumping up and down and then Dad pretended he was a dolphin and I rode on his back.

I found a special birthday present for Bella in the swimming pool shop too. Some super-cool turquoise goggles so that she could see under water. I didn't need goggles myself because I didn't actually like going under water.

I was still a bit worried about swimming even after my special practice with Dad – but it was fine on Bella's birthday. Emily wasn't very good at swimming either, so most of the time we paddled by the fountains and the plastic palms and played we were shipwrecked on a desert island. Chloe was too busy showing off how far and how fast she could swim to bother about us. Amy was quite good at swimming too, but Bella was the best. She really was brilliant. Bella's dad called her his little water-baby. Bella wasn't exactly *little* but she was certainly a star at swimming. She especially loved swimming under water. So my turquoise-goggles birthday present was a big success!

When Bella's dad drove us all back to Bella's house we found Bella's mum had her birthday tea all ready for us. It was a HUGE tea. There were six different kinds of sandwiches: egg mayonnaise; chicken; prawn; banana and cream cheese; bacon, lettuce and tomato; and peanut butter and grape jelly. There were six different kinds of cake too: alphabet fairy cakes; chocolate crispies; chocolate fudge cake; blackcurrant cheesecake; carrot cake; and the special ginormous swimming-pool birthday cake. It had five little marzipan girls in swimming costumes standing in the middle.

It was the most special birthday cake in the world. If I'd been Bella I wouldn't have wanted to eat it, I'd have wanted to keep it for ever.

Bella and I are very different. She cut it all up with a special cake knife and ate two huge slices straight off, and *all* the little marzipan girls.

'Wait till you see *my* birthday cake,' said Chloe.

'What's it going to be like?' said Emily.

'*Aha!*' said Chloe.

I was *sick* of Chloe. I was starting to worry about the sleepover part of this party. I was sure I'd be the one left out again. But guess what, guess what, guess what! Bella's mum and dad moved into the spare room. Bella and Amy and Chloe and Emily and I got to sleep in their great big double bed, all of us in together!

It was the greatest fun ever. I was on the outside but I had Emily next to me. I secretly tucked Midnight in the other side, under the covers. We all got the most terrible giggles so that the whole bed wobbled. Bella had a big box of birthday chocolates and kept passing them round. Emily didn't have any. I had two. Amy had three. Chloe had five. Bella had *thirteen*!

We didn't settle down to sleep for ages – and then we got the giggles again because whenever one of us turned over we all had to. Midnight turned too and Emily felt his furry paws. She gave him a special cuddle.

'He's so sweet,' she whispered in my ear. 'I've got a little teddy called Buttercup. Well, he was a present for my baby brother but *he* just chews his fur so Buttercup's mine now. You'll see him when you come to my house for *my* sleepover party. *If* my mum lets me have one.'

☆ CHAPTER SIX ☆

Emily's mum *did* let her have a sleepover party.

'You're all invited, of course,' she said. 'There's too much baby junk in our dining room to have a proper party tea so Mum says we can all go out for a picnic. I hope that's OK?' Emily looked a little anxious.

'It's more than OK. It's a simply great idea. I *love* picnics,' I said. We didn't go on many picnics ourselves because Lily got upset anywhere strange and could only eat properly in her special chair with straps.

'I like picnics too,' said Amy.

'Me too. Yum yum. I especially love picnic food,' said Bella.

We all looked a little anxiously at Chloe.

'A picnic is a good idea,' said Chloe. 'Though wait till you find out my idea for *my* sleepover party.'

'Do tell us, Chloe,' Emily begged.

But Chloe just went, 'Aha.' I was starting to think she was just doing it to annoy. Maybe she didn't have any ideas at all, good or bad.

Chloe saw me staring at her.

'What about *your* sleepover party, Daisy?' she said.

'What about it?' I said weakly.

'Well, have you got it all sorted out yet?'

'Oh . . . yes. Well. Sort of,' I said. 'I don't know a hundred per cent if I can *have* my own sleepover party.'

'Don't you worry about it, Daisy,' said Emily. 'I had to beg and beg and beg before my mum said yes.'

'But it won't be fair if Daisy doesn't have a sleepover party. She's been to Amy's and Bella's. She's coming to Emily's. And she might be coming to mine. *If* I invite her. So she's *got* to have one herself. Otherwise she can't be in our Alphabet Girls club and go round with us,' said Chloe.

'That's not fair,' I said. 'It was me that *invented* the Alphabet Girls.'

'Well, it's a stupid club anyway. We don't really *do* anything,' said Chloe.

I was furious. I'd been absolutely brimming over with ideas for things we could do. I'd studied the special alphabet signing language for deaf people (there were all these hand diagrams in my dad's old diary) and I'd tried to teach them to the others so we could have our own secret alphabet language. But Chloe got bored after two minutes and wouldn't try. She wouldn't let the others learn either. I'd suggested we write letters to each other and every time a word contained *our* letter we'd write it in a special colour. Guess what. Chloe said this was too fiddly, and pointless anyway. So *then* I suggested we have a competition where we all had shoe boxes and we had to collect in it as many 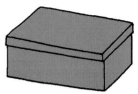 things as possible beginning with our own letter. The one who got the most would get a prize. I even spent my own pocket money on the prize, a special shiny notebook with ABCs all over the cover.

Amy and Bella and Emily thought this the best idea ever. Chloe said it *might* be fun. I was pretty proud of this idea myself. I really hoped *I* might get the notebook. I collected Dad's diary and a tiny doll and a drawing pin and a little china dog and

dental floss and a Disprin and a dandelion and a mini-doughnut and a plastic dinosaur and a sparkly glass ring like a diamond. So things were looking good. But Chloe spoilt it all. She filled her shoebox to the brim with chocolate buttons. She must have bought bags and bags of them.

'There are hundreds and hundreds of chocolates!' she said. 'So I've won. Give us the notebook then.'

'But they are meant to be all *different* things,' I said.

'You didn't say so,' said Chloe.

'I thought it was obvious.'

'It's obvious *you're* just a bad loser,' said Chloe. 'I want my notebook!'

So I had to give it to her, even though Emily and Amy agreed it wasn't really fair. Bella was too busy helping herself to Chloe's chocolates to comment.

I couldn't stick Chloe. I decided that I didn't *want* to go to her sleepover party. But I very, very badly wanted to go to Emily's. I tried so hard to think of a good birthday present for her. Mum took me shopping on Saturday morning and I spent ages and ages and ages looking at pens and crayons and books but nothing seemed *special* enough for Emily.

Lily was in a good mood at first and slumped to one side, daydreaming, but after an hour she started fussing. Loudly.

'Shut *up*, Lily,' I hissed. 'Why do you *always* have to spoil things?'

'Hey, hey!' said Mum. 'It's not Lily's fault. And she's been really really sweet today. *You're* the one who's grumpy.'

'Well, I can't *choose*,' I said, nearly in tears. 'And Emily's party is this afternoon. I can't be the only one not giving her a present.'

'All these birthday presents!' said Mum. 'It's getting a bit much. Still, I suppose it's *your* birthday soon. Are you still keen on this sleepover idea, Daisy?'

'Yes. No. I don't know,' I said.

I didn't want to think about my birthday. I wanted to think about Emily's. I was so looking forward to going to her house – and she had said she'd show me her little teddy, Buttercup.

'I've had an idea!' I said.

We went down to the toy department. I searched along a whole shelf of teddy bears. There were great big growly ones, tiny baby ones, plump teddies in silk waistcoats, soft teddies with velvet paws, smiley teddies and sad teddies and silly teddies with goofy faces.

And right at the very end of the row was a little girl teddy. She had pink fur and a little blue pinafore frock embroidered with a tiny white flower.

'She's *perfect* for Emily's birthday present!' I said.

☆ CHAPTER SEVEN ☆

Emily loved her bear. She gave me a big hug.

'A bear hug!' she said. 'Oh Daisy, she's so sweet. And look, she's got a daisy on her pinafore. I'll *call* her Daisy.'

'I think teddies are stupid,' said Chloe. 'They're for *babies*.'

Chloe gave Emily a special CD album of girl singers. She left the price on to show it was very expensive. Emily gave her a hug too. Emily gave everyone a hug. She was so happy she got very pink in the face. She matched Daisy Bear's fur.

Chloe suggested Emily play her new CD so we could all dance but Emily's mum said she'd sooner we didn't play music just at the moment as Emily's little brother Ben was having a nap, and there wasn't really space for us to dance, so perhaps we could all go out in the garden for half an hour while she got the picnic ready.

So we went into the garden with Emily's dad and played football. Emily got to pick her team first as it was her birthday. She picked Chloe and me. Emily's dad went on Amy and Bella's team but guess what – we still beat them! Emily is very good at football and Chloe is very good at barging into people to stop them getting the ball and, although it sounds like showing off, *I* happen to be very good at football too.

'We are the champions!' Emily and Chloe and I sang, and we jumped up and down and hugged each other every time we scored a goal. It felt very strange hugging Chloe. Maybe we were proper friends now.

Maybe not. When we were setting off for the picnic Emily suggested I fetch Midnight while she got her Buttercup and brand-new Daisy.

'Yuck! What do you want *them* for?' said Chloe.

'It's a *picnic*, Chloe!' said Emily.

'A teddy bear's picnic!' I said.

We both started singing that funny old teddy bear's picnic song. Amy joined in. Bella joined in.

We sang it in the car. Emily's mum and dad joined in. Emily's baby brother Ben tried to join in. Chloe didn't even try. She sat scowling and sighing and muttering that we were all dead babyish.

When we got out of the car at the park Chloe suddenly gave me a push so that I fell on my knees and got my new trousers all dirty. It hurt too. I tried very hard indeed not to cry.

'Did you push Daisy, Chloe?' said Emily's mum.

'No, of course not. I was just helping her out of the car. It was an accident,' said Chloe.

It was accidentally *on purpose.* I hid my face in Midnight's fur.

'Oh, look at little diddums with her teddy-weddy,' Chloe muttered.

I wished Midnight was a real bear and could bite her.

We had another game of football but my knees were bleeding and sticking to my trousers so it was too sore to run. I couldn't be on a team. I had to sit on a rug beside Emily's mum and her little brother Ben.

Still, that wasn't so bad. Ben got a bit grizzly so Emily's mum let me give him his bottle. I am very used to helping people drink. I know exactly the right angle.

'You're just like a little mum, Daisy,' said Emily's mum. 'Have you got a little brother at home?'

'No, I've just got . . . my sister,' I said, sitting Ben up and burping him.

'Is she still a baby?' said Emily's mum.

'Not really,' I said, vaguely.

'Well, anyway, I'm very glad you and Emily have made friends. You must come round and play whenever you want. You'd be very welcome.'

I was so happy I gave Baby Ben a big kiss on his button nose.

Emily's mum was frowning over at Chloe who was stamping her foot and complaining because Amy and Bella had managed to score a goal. She didn't look as if Chloe was very welcome at all!

I gave a great grin. Emily smiled back at me and came running over. 'How are your poor knees, Daisy?' she said.

'*Emily!* Come back. You're the *goalie!*' Chloe screeched.

'I'm not playing any more. It's not really fair playing football when Daisy can't join in,' said Emily.

'Anyway, now that we've got Ben fed I think it's time for our picnic,' said Emily's mum quickly, before Chloe could make any further fuss.

The picnic was *delicious*: chicken drumsticks and tiny tomatoes and crusty French bread and crisps and apples and cherry flapjacks

and a yellow birthday cake in the shape of a teddy bear! Emily insisted Daisy Bear and Buttercup and Midnight all had tiny slices too.

'I wish I'd brought *my* teddy along,' said Bella. 'This is yummy cake, Emily. Though I think chocolate's still my favourite. You haven't got anything chocolatey at all.'

'I've gone off chocolate,' said Emily firmly.

She seemed to have gone off Chloe too! When we got changed into our pyjamas back at Emily's house it hurt pulling my trousers off and my knees bled a bit. Emily looked shocked.

'Your poor knees, Daisy,' she said. She looked hard at Chloe. 'Look at the state of Daisy's knees, Chloe,' she said sternly.

Chloe shrugged. 'It was an accident, I *said.*'

'Poor Daisy,' said Bella.

'Yes, you're being ever so brave, Daisy,' said Amy.

Emily put her arm round me while Emily's mum gave my knees a wash and put stingy stuff on them and bandaged them carefully.

'I don't see why everyone's making such a fuss about Daisy's boring old knees,' Chloe muttered. 'They're just scratched, that's all.'

'Do shut up, Chloe,' said Emily.

Then you'll never guess what. Emily said I could share *her* bed for the sleepover. Amy and Bella shared the other bed. And Chloe had to have the spare mattress all by herself.

☆ CHAPTER EIGHT ☆

I was certain Chloe wasn't going to invite me to her sleepover party. Especially now that Emily was very nearly my best friend too.

Chloe had special invitations. They were all different colours. Emily had a red envelope, Bella a blue, Amy an orange. Surprise, surprise. I didn't have an invitation.

'What about Daisy?' said Emily.

'Who?' said Chloe, as if she'd never even heard of me.

'You are funny, Chloe! *Daisy*,' said Emily, putting her arm round me.

'You didn't forget Daisy, did you?' said Amy.

'I didn't forget her,' said Chloe. 'But my mum says I can only have three people at my sleepover party. So that's Emily and Amy and Bella. Right?'

'That's all *wrong*,' said Emily. She was going very pink in the face.

'It's not fair on Daisy,' said Amy.

'Poor Daisy,' said Bella, giving me a squeeze.

'Yes, poor Daisy,' said Chloe, as if she was really sorry. As if!

'Daisy's got to come too, Chloe!' said Emily, getting even pinker.

'Look, it's not *my* fault. It's my *mum*.'

'Your mum lets you do anything you want, you know she does. You're just not being fair,' said Emily.

'It *is* fair, because I've been to your sleepover party, Emily, and I've been to Amy's and I've been to Bella's. I haven't been to Daisy's. She doesn't even know for definite if she's going to have a sleepover party,' said Chloe.

'You're just being *mean*, Chloe,' said Emily.

'Don't you start getting all stroppy with me, Emily, or you won't be coming to my sleepover party either, even if you are my best friend,' said Chloe.

'It's OK, Emily,' I whispered.

'It's *not* OK,' said Emily. 'I don't want to come to your sleepover party if Daisy can't come too.'

She stared very fiercely at Amy and Bella. 'You don't want to either, do you?' she said.

Amy and Bella looked uncertain. But then Bella nodded and said, 'That's right, Emily.'

And Amy nodded too.

Chloe glared at Amy and Bella. She looked as if she might hit Emily. She seemed all set to *murder* me.

'See if I care then,' she said, and she flounced off.

'Oh dear,' said Amy.

'She said she was going to have a gigantic chocolate cake at her party,' said Bella, sighing.

'She's really going to have it in for me now,' said Emily. 'You know what she can be like. I've tried and tried to stop being friends with Chloe – but it's better to have her as your friend than your deadly enemy.'

'It's all my fault!' I said, feeling truly dreadful.

Emily and Bella and Amy were very comforting but I still felt bad. I didn't tell Mum when I got home from school. I didn't tell Dad when he got home from work.

I waited until it was bedtime and then I crept into Lily's bed and cuddled up with her and told her all about it.

Lily went, 'Ur ur ur ur ur.'

I decided that was Lily-language for, 'That Chloe is a mean hateful pig.'

'I'm scared she'll be really, really horrible now,' I whispered. 'I'm *used* to her being mean to me. But it'll be so awful if she's mean to Emily too.'

Lily went, 'Ur ur ur ur ur,' as if she were saying, 'Don't you worry about it, Daisy.'

I did worry. Lots and lots. I didn't sleep much that night. But guess what? Chloe dropped a pink envelope on my desk in the morning.

'I got my mum to change her mind,' she said. 'You're coming to my sleepover party now, Daisy. And you, Emily. And Bella and Amy.'

'Oh *great*, Chloe!' said Emily, and she gave her a big hug. 'Isn't that wonderful, Daisy?'

I wasn't sure.

I was even less sure when Chloe whispered in my ear, 'I don't *really* want you to come, Daisy Diddums.'

I didn't want to get Chloe a birthday present. Especially a birthday present she'd really, really like. But when Dad and I went down the video shop on Friday night they were having a special sale and there was this video called 'The Spooky Sleepover' and I knew it would be just perfect for Chloe.

Mum was a bit cross with Dad for buying it. 'It's much too scary for a little girl,' she said.

'It sounds like this Chloe is much scarier than any soppy video,' said Dad.

He took me to the party on Saturday because he said he couldn't wait to meet Chloe. He looked a bit taken aback when he saw her. Chloe is little and cute and she's got big blue eyes and these blonde curls. It's pretty sickening actually.

Chloe gave me this great big false smile when my dad was still there.

'Ooh, what a super-sounding video! I hope it's not too frightening. Thank you ever so much, Daisy,' said Chloe.

But the second Dad was gone Chloe stuck her tongue out at me and dropped the video on the floor.

'I saw this ages ago and it sucks. It isn't spooky at all. Trust you to pick a *baby* film, Daisy Diddums.'

☆ CHAPTER NINE ☆

'Come on, Diddums,' said Chloe. 'We're all in the kitchen. I suppose you'd better come too.'

Chloe's kitchen was amazingly big and posh and shiny with all sorts of cupboards and ovens and machines. Chloe's mum was as shiny as her kitchen. She wore a white glittery top and white satin trousers, with a little pink-and-white frilly apron over the top. She looked more like Chloe's sister than her mum.

Emily and Amy and Bella were all standing at a crowded table with big aprons pinned around them and their sleeves rolled up.

'Hi, Daisy!' said Emily. 'We're all making our own pizzas – it's such fun.'

'We can choose any topping we like,' said Amy, arranging pepperoni in a noughts and crosses shape on her pizza.

'I'm making a Bellaroni special,' Bella giggled, squirting chocolate sauce everywhere.

'See, I *said* I was going to have a brilliant sleepover party,' said Chloe. 'The best in the whole world.'

'For the best little girl in the whole world,' said Chloe's dad, popping his head round the door.

Chloe's mum was very young, but Chloe's dad was quite old, with a bald head and a big fat tummy. He made a pizza too – with *all* the toppings.

'Wow!' said Bella, seriously impressed.

'What are you going to put on your pizza, Daisy?' asked Emily.

I thought hard.

'I'm going to make mine a face,' I said.

I sprinkled lots of grated cheese on the top half for hair. Then I did olives for eyes and a slice of yellow pepper for a nose and a curvy red pepper slice for a smiley mouth. I placed a tomato each side for rosy cheeks and I used pineapple chunks for gold earrings and a choker necklace.

'Oh Daisy, you are *clever*,' said Emily.

'It looks so good you won't want to eat it,' said Bella.

'How about a couple of anchovies for eyebrows?' said Amy.

'No! They'd look good but I hate anchovies,' I said. I think they look like grey slimy worms. They always give me the shudders.

Chloe didn't say anything. But when we all followed Chloe's dad into their dining room Chloe hung back to help her mum put the pizzas into the giant oven.

Chloe's dad pretended to be a barman and fixed us all a fruit-juice cocktail. They didn't just have little paper umbrellas like at Amy's. They had tiny plastic Mickey Mouse stirrers and cherries on sticks and ice-cubes in the shape of stars.

We all clinked glasses and when Chloe came into the dining room we sang *Happy Birthday*. Chloe's dad conducted us and got all watery-eyed at the end. Then he seated us at the dining table. We each had a little present on our side plate. It was a little letter charm on a silvery bracelet. A B C D and E. Chloe's C was gold and her bracelet was a proper gold link one with little golden hearts.

'Real gold for our birthday girl,' said her dad.

'And look, I've got real gold heart earrings to match,' said Chloe, looping her curls behind her ears. 'I had them pierced as an extra birthday present.'

We all stared at her ears enviously. My mum says I'm going to have to wait right up until I'm *sixteen* before I'm allowed to have my ears pierced.

Chloe's mum came in with the first two pizzas.

She'd taken her apron off. Her T-shirt top was so tiny it showed her bare tummy and she'd had her belly button pierced! It looked truly cool. I hadn't realized mums could have curvy waists and flat tummies. My mum hasn't.

Chloe's mum served Chloe and Emily with their pizzas.

Then she fetched Amy's and Bella's.

'Are you sure you meant to use *chocolate* sauce, Bella?' said Chloe's mum, putting Bella's very brown pizza in front of her.

'Oh yes, yummy! Chocolate's my favourite thing in all the world,' said Bella happily.

'Well, I'll fetch you some chocolate drops to put on top, if you like,' said Chloe's mum, laughing.

She was joking but Bella said, 'Yes, please!'

Chloe's mum went to get Bella some chocolate drops – and she brought my pizza too.

'You must love anchovies even more than Bella loves chocolate, Daisy,' said Chloe's mum.

I stared at her. I stared at my pizza. There was still a face with cheesy hair and olive eyes and a pepper mouth. But all the plain skin gaps in between were filled in with grey slimy anchovies. Hundreds of them!

'It looks very effective, my love, but I'm really not sure you should eat so many anchovies. You'll make yourself sick,' said Chloe's mum.

'I – I don't like anchovies,' I whispered.

'Then why on earth put them on your pizza?' said Chloe, snorting with laughter.

I hadn't put them on my pizza.

I knew who *had*.

It must have been Chloe herself. But I couldn't say anything at her own party. And Chloe's mum and dad wouldn't have believed me anyway. They thought Chloe was the best little girl in the world. I knew she was the *worst*.

I tried to eat the cheesy hair on my pizza but the anchovies had even got under there. It was as if they were still alive and had wriggled everywhere. I couldn't swallow a mouthful.

'That was a bit of a waste, Daisy,' said Chloe's mum. 'Still, never mind. I'm sure you can fill up on Chloe's birthday cake.'

Chloe had the biggest cake in the whole world. It was in three tiers, just like a wedding cake. The bottom layer was fruit cake with extra cherries and bright yellow marzipan under the white icing.

The middle layer was chocolate fudge cake with lots of chocolate buttercream. The top layer was vanilla sponge with strawberry jam and fresh cream. It had HAPPY BIRTHDAY, CHLOE, SWEETHEART in silver iced writing with silver hearts studded all around the edge.

'We'll make sure *your* slice has a special anchovy filling, Daisy,' Chloe whispered.

I think she might have been joking this time.

But I couldn't take any chances. I didn't eat a bite of this most beautiful birthday cake. I sat and watched the others eating it. (Bella had a big slice from each layer.)

I felt my lips go trembly and my eyes starting pricking but I was absolutely determined not to cry in front of Chloe.

I didn't cry later on when we all went up to Chloe's bedroom and I saw I'd been put in a sleeping bag all by myself over by the door.

I didn't cry when we all watched a scary horror movie on Chloe's television about an evil child with a teddy bear possessed by the devil. He smothered all these little kids but he ended up being horribly ripped to bits. I was very glad Midnight was still zipped up in my overnight bag or *he* might have cried.

I didn't cry when we all got ready for bed and it was my turn in the loo and the lock didn't work properly and Chloe suddenly opened the door on me and everyone laughed.

I didn't cry when we all got into bed (I got into bag) and we watched a much, much, much scarier horror movie about a witchy white ghost who crept up on these girls in a college dormitory and murdered them one by one.

'This is *too* scary, Chloe,' Emily said.

'It's like it's *real*,' said Amy, sucking her thumb.

'Can't we watch some other movie?' said Bella. 'I'm not going to be able to sleep for worrying about the witchy white ghost.'

'It's OK,' said Chloe. 'If the witchy white ghost comes creeping up on us she'll get Daisy first as she's the one nearest the door! And anyway, you don't *sleep* at a sleepover party.'

I certainly didn't sleep. I stayed awake all night long, hunched into a ball in my sleeping bag, clutching Midnight tight. But then he nearly turned into Devil Bear and wanted to smother me. I had to grip him in my knees. They were right up under my chin because there might be anchovies wriggling round the bottom of the sleeping bag. And all the time the witchy white ghost wailed just outside the bedroom door, waiting to come and get me . . .

☆ CHAPTER TEN ☆

'Not long now till your birthday, Daisy,' said Mum.
I didn't say anything.

Lily went, 'Ur ur ur ur ur.' She was lying on the rug and I was tickling her.

'I suppose you want to have a sleepover party too,' said Mum.

I didn't say anything.

Lily went, 'UR UR UR UR UR!'

'Daisy! I'm talking to you! And stop tickling Lily.'

'She likes it. Don't you, Lily?' I said.

'URRR URRR URRR URRR URRR!'

'She'll get over-excited. Stop it, now.'

'URRRRRRRRRR! URRRRRRRRRR!'

Lily got so over-excited she started wailing and wouldn't stop. She cried until she was sick. Mum had to take her upstairs to change her and calm her down.

Lily's wails were very weak and tired now. At least she always slept for ages after one of her bad crying fits. At last she went quiet.

It was very quiet in the living room too. I looked at Dad. I thought he was cross with me. He switched on the television. Then he switched it off. He patted his knee.

'Want to come and have a cuddle?' he said.

I was surprised but very pleased. I tucked in beside Dad and he put his arm round me and kissed the top of my head. Then he pretended he was a sheep and my hair was grass so he went gobble gobble munch munch.

'I love this game. We haven't played it for ages!' I said.

'I'll try to get home from work early more often,' Dad said. 'I don't get to see enough of you, Daisy. And poor Mum is always so busy with Lily.'

'Yes,' I said, sighing. 'Sorry I made her get upset,' I added in a tiny voice.

'That's OK, pet. You were only playing,' said Dad.

'Yes, but I was playing a bit too much,' I said.

'Don't let's talk about Lily. Let's talk about you – and this birthday of yours,' said Dad.

I didn't say anything.

'What's up?'

'Nothing,' I said.

'Nothing!' said Dad. 'Maybe I'm going to start tickling *you* unless you tell me what's making you look so worried. Come on, my little glum chum.' He tickled me under my chin and I collapsed, squeaking and spluttering.

'Don't! Please don't!'

'Well, tell me what's the matter.'

'There's nothing the matter, Dad, honest. It's just . . . I don't really want a sleepover party for my birthday.'

'But I thought they were all the rage. Just recently you've been to heaps.'

'I know.'

'So you really need to invite everyone back.'

'But . . . I don't want to.'

'Why?'

I fidgeted.

Dad put his head close to mine.

'Is it because of Lily?' he whispered.

'A bit,' I whispered back.

'We'll explain about Lily to your friends.'

'But they might still be a bit funny about it. Not Emily. She's ever so special. And Bella's lovely too. And Amy. It's just . . . Chloe. Chloe's *horrible.*'

'The little curly-haired one?' said Dad.

'Her,' I said grimly.

'Oh well, it's easy-peasy,' said Dad. 'Invite Emily and Bella and Amy to your sleepover birthday party and leave Chloe out.'

'*Really?*'

'Of course. It's your birthday. You don't have to invite anyone you don't want,' said Dad.

'But Emily and Amy and Bella said it wasn't fair when Chloe tried not to invite me to *her* sleepover.'

'Do they all like Chloe?'

'Well . . . I think they're just a bit scared of her.'

'Then they'll probably be glad she's not invited,' said Dad.

'I'll be ever so, ever so glad!' I said, bouncing up and down on Dad's knee.

'That's it, little Smiley-Face. All settled,' said Dad, beaming.

But it wasn't settled.

Mum said I had to invite Chloe too.

'It's only fair. You went to Chloe's party, Daisy, so she has to come to yours.'

'But she didn't want me to come, Mum! She tried hard *not* to invite me. She's really mean to me, Mum. She gangs up on me 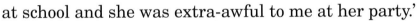 at school and she was extra-awful to me at her party.'

'Why didn't you tell me?'

'I *am* telling you!'

'No, at the time, silly.'

'You were busy with Lily. You're *always* busy with Lily.'

'No, I'm not. Not always. Anyway, I'm afraid I've already invited Chloe. Her mother rang up after her party because she was worried you might be sickening for something. She said you didn't eat anything, poppet.'

'Ha! Chloe put anchovies all over my pizza!'

I shuddered so hard I nearly fell out of Dad's armchair.

'Oh dear. Well, I told Chloe's mum you'd be having a sleepover party yourself and I automatically invited Chloe.'

'Can't we un-invite this foul little girl?' said Dad, giving me a hug.

'Not really. It would look awful.'

'*She's* awful.'

'She won't be able to be awful to you at our house, not when it's your special party, Daisy.'

I was sure Chloe would find a way.

I didn't say any more to Dad. I didn't say any more to Mum. But after they were asleep I crept into bed beside Lily. She'd been asleep for hours and hours but she was awake now. 'I hate Chloe,' I said.

'Ur ur ur ur ur,' said Lily, comfortingly, as if she hated her too.

'She's so mean to me,' I said.

'Ur ur ur ur ur,' said Lily.

I thought for a little while.

'I'm sometimes mean to you, Lily,' I said. 'Do you hate me sometimes?'

'Ur ur ur ur ur,' said Lily. 'Ur ur ur ur *ur*.'

I hoped she was saying she didn't hate me at all, she loved me because I was her sister.

'Well, I love you because you're *my* sister, Lily,' I said. 'And if Chloe is mean to you I'll smack her hard, you just wait and see.'

☆ CHAPTER ELEVEN ☆

Mum and Dad sang *Happy Birthday* to me on Saturday morning. Lily sang too, screeching louder and louder: 'UR UR UR UR UR!'

'She's getting over-excited again, Mum,' I said.

'Never mind,' said Mum.

'We're *all* over-excited because it's your birthday, Daisy,' said Dad.

I had a special birthday breakfast of croissants and cherry jam and hot chocolate – yummy yummy.

'Do you think we can have more hot chocolate later on for my party?' I said. 'I think Bella would like it a lot.'

'Yes, of course,' said Mum.

'But Emily doesn't like chocolate any more,' I worried.

'We'll find something else for Emily.'

'Something special – because Emily's my almost best friend,' I said.

'What shall we serve Chloe?' said Dad, winking. 'A mug of greasy lukewarm washing-up water?'

I fell about laughing. Mum frowned, but she couldn't stop herself giggling too.

After breakfast Mum got Lily ready and then Dad took her for a long walk in her wheelchair while Mum and I cleared up and then made my birthday cake together. Mum let me stir the mixture and spoon it out into the cake tin. She let me scrape the mixing bowl with the spoon (and then my finger and *then* my tongue!). We made white chocolate crunch biscuits while the cake was cooling and *then* we did the decorating.

Mum got a very sharp knife and started cutting the cake.

'Mum! *I* cut the cake. It's my birthday. What are you doing? The cake isn't even finished yet.'

'I know. I am finishing it. I'm turning it into a special cake,' said Mum. 'Watch.'

I watched. Mum cut delicate little wedges out of the cake every so often. She was turning the cake into a particular shape. Then I suddenly realized.

'It's a *daisy*! Oh Mum, how brilliant!'

Mum defined each petal perfectly. Then we mixed up some bright white icing and carefully covered it all over.

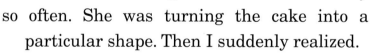

'It looks lovely!' I said, putting a little smear of icing on one of the cut-off wedges. 'Yum! It tastes lovely too.'

'It's not quite finished yet,' said Mum.

She coloured the left-over icing yellow and spread that in a neat circle in the middle so that the cake looked just like a real daisy. When it was all dry she iced HAPPY BIRTHDAY DAISY in pink on top. It looked *so* beautiful, especially when Mum slid the cake onto our best green 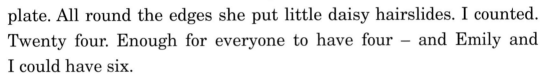 plate. All round the edges she put little daisy hairslides. I counted. Twenty four. Enough for everyone to have four – and Emily and I could have six.

'No, no, four each,' said Mum.

'Emily, me, Bella, Amy and Chloe, yuck yuck. Five times four is twenty.'

'There are six of you, silly. What about Lily?' said Mum.

'But Lily isn't part of the sleepover party,' I said.

'Of course she is! She's your sister.'

'Lily can't do her own hair so she doesn't need hairslides.'

'You could do her hair for her. And I'm sure she'll love her daisy hairslides,' said Mum. 'Oh, there's Lily and Dad back now. Did you have a lovely walk, Lily? What's all that silly noise for?'

'UR UR UR UR UR!' Lily wailed.

'I took her round the shopping centre. I thought she'd like those giant teddies. *Big* mistake,' said Dad, mopping his brow.

'Oh yes, she's scared of them,' said Mum, sighing.

'Well, you could have told me,' said Dad.

'Lily's been scared of them for ages,' I said. 'Oh, Dad, you know she doesn't even like my teddy, Midnight.'

'Come on, Lily, let's mop those weepy eyes and wipe that poor nose,' said Mum. 'And stop that noise, *please*!'

'Ur ur ur ur ur,' Lily mumbled, sniffling.

Mum started to carry Lily upstairs.

'Oh dear, she needs changing too. Look, you two had better get started on Daisy's bedroom. Though how all five girls are going to squash in there I just don't know.'

'Lots of girls use the living room for sleepovers,' I suggested.

'There's even less space in our living room,' said Dad, 'what with Lily's special chair and her rug and all her other stuff.' Then he looked at the window. He looked out of the window.

'I know!' said Dad. 'Daisy, how about having your sleepover in the garden? We could get the tent out of the loft.'

'Oh Dad! Magic!' I said.

We went racing up the stairs past Mum and Lily so that Dad could climb up in the loft. We bought all the camping stuff last year for our summer holiday. We can't usually stay in a hotel because it's so difficult with Lily. It was difficult camping with her too. She cried most of the night. And the next, even though I got in her sleeping bag with her. She didn't like it because it was different. The third night Lily cried and Mum cried too. Dad didn't cry but he said, 'This is ridiculous,' and we packed up the tent and drove home in the middle of the night.

'I knew that tent would come in useful eventually,' Dad said now, and he unpacked it and took it out into the garden.

'It's going to be so cool!' I said.

'Too cool, literally,' said Mum. 'It'll be freezing cold in the middle of the night.'

'The girls can all wrap up really warmly. They'll have a whale of a time,' said Dad.

'But Lily won't be able to join in any of the fun. You know what she's like in that tent,' said Mum.

'You don't have to remind me!' said Dad.

I didn't say anything.

I couldn't help feeling very glad indeed that Lily wouldn't be able to join in.

☆ CHAPTER TWELVE ☆

I wore my starry T-shirt and my new birthday-present jeans with embroidered daisies up and down the legs. I couldn't wait to have the daisy hairslides in my hair to match.

'You look lovely, Daisy,' said Mum.

'Our special birthday girl,' said Dad.

'Ur ur ur ur ur,' said Lily softly. I wondered if she really knew it was my birthday.

I wondered if she ever knew when it was her birthday. I wondered if Lily wished she could wear tiny T-shirts and embroidered jeans. Lily mostly wore big towelling tops because she dribbled and spilt so much and they stopped her getting too wet. She wore loose jogging trousers because they were easy to whip on and off when she needed changing. Lily's clothes were practical but they weren't *pretty*.

Lily wasn't pretty either. Mum kept her very clean but her face went funny and she always looked lopsided because she couldn't sit up properly. She did have lovely long hair though.

'Wait till after my party, Lily,' I said, giving her a hug. 'We'll play hairdressers and I'll fix your hair with daisy slides. You'll like them. You'll look dead cool in them.'

'Ur ur ur ur ur!' said Lily excitedly.

'Try not to get her too worked up, pet,' Mum said gently.

'We don't want her roaring her head off when your party guests come,' said Dad.

We all waited. We were all a bit worried. I was sure Chloe was going to say something terrible about Lily. And I wasn't sure that Amy and Bella would be ultra-tactful. And maybe even Emily would act oddly about Lily and then what would I do?

My new birthday jeans suddenly seemed much too tight. I had a horrible squeezy feeling in my tummy. I wished I wasn't having a sleepover party. I wished Mum would take Lily and hide her away for the whole weekend.

Amy arrived first. 'Hi, Daisy. Happy birthday!'

She gave me a pink plastic make-up bag with silver nail varnish and a pot of silver face glitter. I was so thrilled I forgot all about Lily for one tiny moment.

'Ur ur ur,' said Lily in the background, determined not to be forgotten.

Amy jumped, startled. She looked at Lily in her special chair.

'That's Lily,' I said. 'She's my sister.'

'Hi, Lily,' Amy said uncertainly.

'Ur ur,' said Lily.

'What's wrong with her?' Amy hissed.

'Something happened to her brain when she was born,' I said.

'Oh dear,' said Amy. 'So can't she walk?'

'No.'

'Well . . . she can sort of talk,' said Amy.

'Yes, she can. And she can shout too!' I said.

I felt a lot, lot, lot better. I *did* like Amy.

Maybe second best to Emily instead of Bella.

Bella arrived next.

'Hello, Daisy. Here, happy birthday!'

She gave me a big box of chocolates with a puppy picture on the lid and a purple ribbon which would come in useful for future hairdressing sessions. Bella glanced at Lily and nodded. Then she looked back at the chocolates. Hopefully.

'Are you going to open them now?' said Bella.

'OK. Oh, they look really yummy!' I said.

I handed the box to Bella.

'You should choose first as it's your birthday,' Bella said, which was good of her, because she was staring hard at the biggest white chocolate in the middle.

'You have that one as you gave them to me,' I said, offering it to her. Bella didn't need persuading. I chose a round chocolate with a rose petal on top. Amy chose a chocolate wrapped in gold paper.

Bella took the box over to Lily.

'Do you want a chocolate?'

'Ur ur ur,' said Lily.

'What did you say?' said Bella.

'Lily can't really say stuff,' I said, going over to her. 'She likes chocolate, but just a weeny bit, so she can't choke.' I broke a tiny piece off my rose chocolate and popped it in Lily's open mouth.

'Poor Lily. Fancy choking on chocolate!' said Bella.

I decided I liked Bella and Amy second-best equal to Emily.

Emily arrived next. She had a star T-shirt on exactly the same as mine! 'Happy birthday, Daisy,' she said. 'Hey, we're the star twins. We can go twinkle twinkle!'

She gave me my birthday present. I felt it first.

It was quite squashy, with a little round bit. The round bit went grur-grur-grur when I squeezed it.

'Ur ur ur !' said Lily excitedly, as if they spoke the same language.

Emily looked surprised. 'Hello,' she said.

'This is Lily,' I said. 'She's my sister.'

'Hi, Lily,' said Emily. She paused. 'I like your hair. I'm trying to grow mine but it's taking *ages*.'

'Ur ur ur,' said Lily. She smiled as if she understood.

I smiled too. I knew Emily was the nicest friend in the whole world.

I unwrapped my birthday present. It was a beautiful new pair of pyjamas, white with yellow buttons and a pattern of little yellow teddy bears and in the pyjama pocket there was a tiny toy teddy.

'He's called Little Growler. Press his tummy!' said Emily. 'That was him growling before. Lily liked it.'

But Lily hadn't realized grur-grur-grur was beartalk. Lily hates bears. She's even scared of tiny teddy bears like Little Growler.

She saw him – and she started. 'UR UR UR UR UR!' Lily wailed.

'Oh goodness, what's the matter?' said Emily.

'UR UR UR UR UR!' Lily screamed.

'What's the matter?' said Amy.

'Has she hurt herself?' said Bella.

'She's just a bit frightened. She'll be all right in a minute,' I said. But she wasn't.

Mum had to cart Lily upstairs to calm her down. Lily wouldn't calm down one bit. She roared.

We heard her being sick.

'Oh dear,' said Emily. 'Will she be all right now?'

'I think she'll need to go to sleep for a while,' said Dad.

We listened. Lily's cries were getting weaker.

'Poor Lily, she'll miss all the fun,' said Amy.

'She'll miss her tea if she goes to sleep,' said Bella.

I crossed my fingers. I hoped Lily would sleep for hours and hours and hours.

☆ CHAPTER THIRTEEN ☆

Chloe was so late I began to think she wasn't coming. My heart started thumping under my twinkle-star T-shirt. My sleepover party would be just for four. Amy and Bella – and Emily and me! Emily might be *my* best friend. I felt I was flying right up to the real stars.

But then I came down to earth with a bump. There was a knock at the door. Chloe was here.

'Happy birthday, Daisy,' she cooed, all smiles in front of her mum. (*My* mum was still upstairs sorting out Lily.)

Chloe had a new T-shirt on too. It had sparkly pink lettering. It said: *The Bestest Little Girl in all the World*. Chloe had pink sparkles on her cheeks and pink lipstick and pink strappy shoes with real heels.

Her present was wrapped up in sparkly pink paper too. I opened it gingerly. I was expecting a parcel of anchovies. But it was a video. It had *101 Dalmatians* on the cover. But 101 Doubts rushed round my head like little dogs. I didn't trust Chloe. Not one bit.

We went into the living room to play. Mum had tried to tidy it up but Lily's special bouncy chair was still there.

'What a weird chair!' said Chloe.

'It's my sister's,' I said.

'But it's ginormous. She must be a *huge* baby.' Chloe blew out her cheeks and waddled like a giant toddler. 'Where is she then? Has she crawled off somewhere?' said Chloe, pretending to look under the table.

'She's upstairs with my mum. She's putting her to bed because she got over-excited.'

'Oh, poor little baba. You'd better watch out, Daisy Diddums. You might get over-excited and put to bed too,' said Chloe. She paused. 'Well, what are we going to do, then?'

I hadn't quite sorted it out.

'Let's dance,' said Amy.

But I didn't have the right sort of music.

'Yuck, this is all baby stuff – or ancient,' said Chloe, flipping through our CDs.

'Maybe we can have tea now?' said Bella. But it was still a bit early for tea, and anyway, Mum was still upstairs with Lily.

'Shall we go out in the garden and play football?' said Emily.

So we went out in the garden, but nearly all the grass was taken up with the tent. Dad was just sorting out the last few tent pegs, hitting them with a wooden mallet.

'Hi, girls!' he said.

'Ooh, a tent!' said Emily.

'I've always wanted to go camping,' said Amy.

'Can we have campfire food?' said Bella.

'We can't play football with that stupid tent there. Shame you've got such a *little* garden.'

'Ah, it's Daisy's special friend Chloe,' said Dad, giving her a funny smile. 'Are you having fun, girls?'

'Yes,' said Emily politely.

'No,' said Chloe.

'We don't know what to do, Dad,' I said desperately.

'Ah. I think Mum was going to sort you girls out before tea – but she's still with Lily, is she? Tell you what! Why don't you play party games?'

'Party games? Like what?' I said.

'Like, *boring*,' said Chloe.

'No, no, they're good fun,' Dad insisted. 'Let's all go indoors and play.'

When Chloe turned to go Dad mimed hitting her over the head with his wooden mallet. Emily and Amy and Bella and I all fell about laughing.

'What's so funny?' said Chloe crossly.

'Nothing. We're just having fun,' I said.

And we *did* have fun. Dad showed us how to play all these weird old-fashioned party games like Squeak Piggy Squeak. When Chloe was the pig she sat on my lap so hard I squeaked for real but I didn't care.

Then we played Stations and I was Clapham Junction and Emily was Vauxhall and we had to keep swapping and once we bumped into each other and got the giggles. Chloe was Waterloo and she bumped into me on purpose and stamped on my toe but I didn't care.

Then we played Murder in the Dark and I got a bit worried Chloe would be the murderer and if she pretended to murder me it might hurt rather a lot. Luckily Bella was the murderer and she just gave me a tiny poke in the tummy and whispered, 'Ever so sorry but you're dead now, Daisy.' Chloe kept pretending to trip over me all the time I was the Dead Body and each time she tripped she kicked. I tried hard not to care.

Dad saw one time and said, 'Hey, Chloe, don't kick Daisy like that!'

Chloe went red as she's not used to being told off.

'I'm sick of playing this silly game. Let's do something else,' she said.

So we played Musical Bumps. It was great fun. Even Chloe cheered up and started jumping to the music, even if it *was* ancient. I wondered if it might start Lily off again but Mum came down at last and muttered to Dad that she was fast asleep.

'So I'll fix tea,' said Mum.

Everyone loved my beautiful Daisy cake.

Mum even cut the sandwiches with a special cutter so they were daisy-shaped too. We drank our lemonade out of green glasses and had little white iced buns and white chocolate clusters and green grape jelly and vanilla ice-cream.

'I love the way it all matches,' said Amy.

'It looks almost too lovely to eat,' said Emily.

'*Almost*,' said Bella, tucking in straight away.

We all tucked in. We ate and ate until we were very nearly full. Then I had to cut my birthday cake ever so carefully. As the knife sliced through the thick icing and soft sponge and gooey jam I made my birthday wish.

'I wish Emily could be my best friend,' I whispered to myself.

Then everyone sang *Happy Birthday To You*. When they got to '*Happy Birthday, dear Daisy*,' Chloe sang '*Diddums Daisy*' but I didn't care.

The birthday cake was delicious. I hoped Mum might make cakes more often! She washed all the daisy hairslides for us because some had got a bit sticky with icing and then she handed them out.

'There are four left over. Can I have them seeing as I've got the longest curliest hair?' said Chloe.

'No, dear, those slides are for Lily,' said Mum.

'Daisy's sister? Babies don't wear hairslides!' said Chloe.

I held my breath. But Bella asked if it would be terribly piggy if she had just one more slice of birthday cake. Dad laughed and offered her the whole plateful.

'I wouldn't do that! She'll eat it all!' said Amy.

'And she doesn't *ever* feel sick,' said Emily.

'You're just a greedy-guts, Bella,' said Chloe. 'You'll grow into a great big whale and never be able to wear decent clothes.'

'Whales don't need clothes. They swim around and spout at silly little tadpoles like you,' said Bella.

She pretended to spout at Chloe, but she still had a large mouthful of cake. Chloe's *Bestest Little Girl in the Whole World* T-shirt got sprayed with crumbs. We all fell about laughing. Chloe didn't find it funny at all.

'You disgusting pig, Bella,' she said, and she pushed her off her chair.

'Hey, hey, that's enough!' said Mum. 'I think it's time you all got down from the table. Daisy, run and find one of your T-shirts, poppet, so Chloe can wear it while I put her own in the washing machine.'

Chloe followed me up the stairs. Amy and Bella and Emily came too. I tiptoed past Lily's door.

'Why are you walking like that?' Chloe asked.

'Shh! Lily's asleep,' I whispered.

Emily and Amy and Bella all started walking on tiptoe too. Chloe went STOMP STOMP CLACKETY CLUMP in her heeled shoes . . . but thank goodness Lily didn't stir in her room.

Everyone squashed into my room.

'Goodness, isn't it weeny?' said Chloe.

'No, it's not,' said Bella.

'It's a lovely room,' said Amy.

'It's the nicest room I've ever seen,' said Emily.

It's not. It *is* weeny. Lily has a proper size bedroom because she's got so much stuff and Mum sometimes sleeps on a campbed beside her if she's having a bad spell. I have to make do with the tiny bedroom – but Dad's put up special shelves on my wall with a roof on top, like a big open dolls' house so all my books and paints and stuff have different 'rooms'. Mum's made me a duvet cover and curtains patterned with dolls' houses and on my window sill I have my real dolls' house. A very tiny family of teddy bears live inside. Midnight is too big but he sometimes likes to squeeze up really small and visit them.

'Dolls' houses are for babies!' said Chloe.

'No, they're not. My gran collects dolls' houses and she's an old lady,' said Emily. 'I'm not really allowed to play with her dolls' houses though.'

'You can play with mine,' I said.

'We're not playing baby doll games,' said Chloe. 'Come on then, Daisy, show me all your T-shirts.'

I showed her my blue T-shirt with the dolphin and my pink T-shirt with little flowers and my black T-shirt with the silver mermaid (only the silver comes off so she hasn't got a tail any more).

'Is this all you've *got*?' said Chloe.

She chose the dolphin T-shirt though she sneered at it and said it was stupid. She had a good look through all my clothes and didn't think much of any of them and she was mean about my shoes too because they came from the wrong shop.

'I wouldn't be seen dead in shoes like that,' she said, throwing herself onto my bed and waggling her wonderful pink strappy heels in the air.

'Can I try your shoes on, Chloe?' said Amy.

Bella tried them on too.

And even Emily.

'Can *I* try them on, Chloe?' I asked.

'No fear. I don't want your smelly old feet in my shoes,' said Chloe.

I wished the dolphin on her T-shirt would swim off with her to the bottom of the sea – and then leave her there, with her head in the sand and her legs in their pink strappy shoes waving in the air.

☆ CHAPTER FOURTEEN ☆

When we went downstairs – Emily, Bella, Amy and me tip-toeing, Chloe clackety-stomping – Mum and Dad were in the kitchen having *their* tea.

'Are we going to play some more Musical Bumps?' said Amy.

'Boring,' said Chloe.

'Are we going to have some more tea?' said Bella.

'Boring,' said Chloe.

'Are we going to go in the tent now?' said Emily.

'Boring,' said Chloe.

'What would you like to do then, Chloe?' said Mum.

'It's Daisy's birthday. She should choose,' said Dad.

'I know!' Mum said quickly. 'Why don't you all go and watch the video Chloe gave Daisy for her birthday? *101 Dalmatians* is a lovely film.'

We went into the living room. Chloe carefully shut the door behind us and then slotted the video into our player. We started to watch.

It wasn't a lovely film. It wasn't *101 Dalmatians*.

It was another white witchy ghost movie. This one was even worse. It's about a girl walking in the country by herself. She keeps looking round anxiously and you hear these footsteps and then there's this awful waily breathing noise, a bit like Lily having one of her spells but worse, so the girl starts to run and she sees this camping site and she runs harder and shouts but then something grabs at her and you see her face and she screams and screams and screams.

I had to suck my thumb hard to stop myself screaming too.

'Look at little suck-a-thumb! *Baby!*' said Chloe. 'She's scared of a silly film.'

'I'm scared too,' said Emily.

'And me,' said Amy.

'Can't we do something else, like see if there's any cake left?' said Bella.

'No, no, you've got to watch the bit that comes next. It's so cool!' said Chloe.

We were at the camping site now. The girl is inside her tent, just waking up and stretching, and then she sees something poking at her tent from the outside and she laughs at first, thinking it's one of her friends. She even calls out to them, but there's no reply, there's just this awful waily noise and then suddenly a terrible white claw rips through the tent and I had to shut my eyes tight and I nearly bit right through my thumb.

'*Watch* it, Daisy. Don't close your eyes!' said Chloe.

'*I* don't want to watch it,' said Bella.

'She doesn't have to watch it if she doesn't want to,' said Amy.

'Shall we switch it off?' said Emily, getting up.

'Sit down, Emily. You're all babies. Of course we're not switching it off,' said Chloe.

But then we heard my Dad calling just outside and Chloe shot up quick and stopped the video. A film on television flashed on instead, just in time.

'How are you doing, girls?' said Dad, putting his head round the door. 'Are you OK, Daisy?'

'Yes, Dad,' I said.

'I thought you were watching *101 Dalmatians*?' said Dad, looking at the television.

'Oh, we *were*. But we just wanted to peek at this film on the telly too,' said Chloe in this cutesy-pie tone she uses for her own dad.

My dad didn't look as if he totally believed her. He blinked at the television.

'Well, I don't think you should be watching this old film. I saw it years ago and it gets a bit scary,' said Dad.

Compared to Chloe's white witchy ghost films it was about as scary as *Teletubbies*, but I was glad when Dad switched the television off, even so.

'Anyway, I've come to announce that your sleeping quarters are now fully prepared, noble ladies,' said Dad in a daft voice, bowing low.

He'd got it beautifully cosy inside the tent, with the big cushions from the sofa to sprawl on and the special garden fairy lights rigged up inside the tent so it glowed precious jewel colours, amber, emerald and ruby. There were lots of our old shawls and rugs and cardies too so that we were still ever so cosy when we were changed into our pyjamas.

Then we talked and talked and talked and talked: about our favourite singers (I copied Emily) and footballers (I copied Emily again) and the boys in our class at school (I didn't need to copy because they're *all* gross). Then we made up our favourite clothes and this time I went first and invented this seriously cool black-and-silver outfit with black high heels and Emily copied *me* because she said she liked the sound of mine so much. We chose our favourite colours (black and silver, naturally) and our favourite animals (Emily and I both said 'bears' together and burst out laughing). Then we all said what we wanted to do when we grew up. Emily said she wanted to be a footballer and if she couldn't she'd teach PE in school and I said I wanted to be an artist but if I couldn't I'd teach Art in school. Chloe said I was a useless copycat which wasn't fair because I've always loved Art and I'm good at teaching too. I teach Lily lots, even though she doesn't learn very quickly. Chloe said teachers were boring anyway and *she* was going to be a famous actress. Amy said she was going to be a famous dancer and Bella said she was going to be a famous TV chef. Then she said she felt a bit peckish and at that *exact* moment Mum came out with big mugs of hot chocolate (and a hot blackcurrant for Emily) and a bowl of popcorn.

'Wow! This is the best sleepover party ever,' said Bella. 'Even better than mine.'

'It's nowhere near as good as mine,' said Chloe.

'We've all had super sleepovers,' said Emily. 'But yours is just great, Daisy,' and she reached for my hand under the rug and gave it a squeeze.

While we sipped our drinks and munched popcorn we swapped our Most Embarrassing Moments (I'm not going to tell you!) and we laughed so much the bowl tipped over and we had to play hunt the popcorn in our sleeping bags. Then we played Double Dare and some of the dares were amazingly outrageous (I'm not going to tell you again, though I will just say that *one* of us took her pyjamas off and went into the garden and ran right round the tent, but it was dark by then so no-one could see – I hope!)

Then we started to tell ghost stories and that was fun at first but Chloe's started to get a bit too scary.

'Do shut up, Chloe,' Emily begged, putting her hands over her ears.

'Don't be stupid. It's just a *story*. Ghosts aren't *real*,' said Chloe.

'Yes, they are! My granny kept seeing the ghost of my grandad after he died,' said Amy.

'Let's *play* ghosts,' said Bella, and she pulled the white pillow case off her pillow and put it over her head and made funny *who-o-o-o* ghost noises. Then she went *oooh* instead because she'd found some more popcorn inside the pillowcase and went gobble gobble munch munch.

'You are a piglet, Bella,' said Amy.

So Bella made piglet noises and then we all played a daft game of Farmyard and got the giggles so badly our tummies hurt. Then we sang all the songs we knew and then we played making up a poem together.

I started it.

'We are the special Alphabet Girls.'

'Some of us have straight hair, some of us have curls,' said Emily.

'We all like to dance if we get the chance,' said Amy.

'We eat lots of chocolate yum yum yum,' said Bella.

'Chloe and Emily, Amy and Bella, and Daisy Diddums Fat Bum,' said Chloe.

'Daisy isn't a bit fat,' said Emily.

'*I* am, but I don't care,' said Bella. 'Daisy, do you think your mum might have some *more* popcorn in the kitchen?'

'I think my mum and dad have gone to bed now. But tell you what we have got . . . my birthday chocolates!'

I handed round the box. Emily said she was far too full up to have even half a chocolate. Amy took one. Chloe chose the special caramel and hazelnut, my favourite. Bella took one – and then another and another – and then even she said sleepily that she was *almost* full up.

We were all starting to feel very, very s-l-e-e-p-y . . .

Bella fell so soundly asleep she started to snore a little bit and we all got the giggles. Then Amy curled up and went quiet. After a long time Chloe dropped off too. Emily and I whispered very, very quietly together. I decided to close my eyes just for a minute and then I was suddenly asleep too . . .

I woke up with a start. I heard this rustling nearby. Then something grabbed hold of my shoulder. The white witchy ghost was coming to get me!

'Help!' I gasped.

'Shut *up*, stupid.'

It was only Chloe, wriggling right out of her sleeping bag.

'What are you *doing*, Chloe? It's still the middle of the night.'

'I know. I need to go to the loo. You'll have to show me where it is.'

'It's upstairs. Mum left the back door ajar so we'd be able to nip in.'

'I won't be able to find it in the dark,' said Chloe, shaking me. 'You'll have to come with me.'

'Oooh, I'm so sleepy, Chloe,' I said. Then a thought occurred to me that made me wake up properly.

'Hey, you're not *scared* of the dark, are you?'

'Of course not, idiot,' said Chloe, but when we crept out into the black garden a cat suddenly yowled and we *both* squealed and clutched each other. We trekked through the wet grass in our bare feet. We were still holding hands.

'You're shaking, Chloe,' I whispered.

'It's cold,' Chloe hissed.

It was cold. But it was also SCARY. I knew it was only my scruffy old garden where I played every day, but in the dark it went wild and woody and I didn't like it one bit. I also felt distinctly weird holding Chloe's hand.

As soon as we got in the house we drew apart abruptly.

'Put the light on now!' said Chloe.

'But I'll wake Mum and Dad,' I said.

I really meant I'd wake Lily. I shushed Chloe and hoped she'd go quietly. At least she wasn't wearing her clackety-stomp high heels.

But Lily was awake already. She obviously felt it was morning now. She heard Chloe and me padding across the dark landing towards the loo. She felt indignant. She wanted to get up too.

'UR UR UR UR UR UR!' Lily wailed.

'A-A-A-A-A-A-H!' Chloe screamed. 'It's the witch ghost!'

'What on earth . . . ?' said Mum, stumbling out of her bedroom.

She switched on the landing light. Chloe was crying! And it wasn't just her face that was damp. She'd wet herself!

She gave a little squeak and hurtled into the bathroom sharpish.

'Oh dear,' said Mum. 'Poor little thing. Look, you see if you can quieten Lily down while I go and find a spare pair of pyjamas for Chloe. You keep out of the way, Daisy, I expect she'll be a bit embarrassed.'

'I'll say!' I muttered.

I went into Lily's room.

'UR UR UR UR UR UR!' said Lily.

'That's right, Lily! You're the greatest. You really frightened her. You're the cleverest sister in the whole wide world.'

☆ CHAPTER FIFTEEN ☆

I went back to the tent – but Chloe didn't. When I woke up in the morning she still wasn't there.

'Where's Chloe?' said Emily, leaning up on one elbow.

'Maybe the witchy ghost has got her!' said Amy, rubbing her eyes.

'I wish!' said Bella. She smacked her lips. 'Is it breakfast time?'

Mum was pouring juice and laying out bowls of cereal in the kitchen. Dad was eating a banana and looking sleepy. Lily was strapped in her special chair. She sang, 'Ur ur ur ur ur,' quietly to herself.

There was no sign of Chloe.

'Did Chloe sleep in my bedroom after . . . ?' I said.

'After what?'

'What happened, Daisy?'

'Tell us!'

'Now, now,' said Mum. 'You don't want to tell tales, Daisy. Chloe decided she wanted to go home so Dad drove her back.'

'In the middle of the night,' said Dad. 'She went all sad and sulky after she wet herself.'

'Dad!' said Mum.

'Oops!' said Dad.

'She *wet* herself?' said Amy.

'*Chloe* wet herself!' said Emily.

'And she calls *us* babies?' said Bella.

We had a wonderful time for the rest of the morning, all five of us. Lily kind of joined in too. Amy gave her a drink of milk and Emily fed her some special cereal and Bella crumbled chocolate into very teeny, tiny pieces and spooned them into Lily's mouth. Lily liked all this attention. She particularly liked the chocolate and went, 'Ur ur ur ur ur,' smacking her lips.

'There. I *knew* she'd like chocolate,' said Bella.

Then we all watched television for a bit and then we played this mad game of Charades. Lily played a baby and an old, old lady and we let her be a ghost again too as she was so very good at it. Then Amy's mum came calling for her. Then Bella's dad. Then for a very special half hour it was just Emily and me and Lily. Emily and I rather wanted to play teddy bears but that was right out of the question, so we played hairdressers instead. I styled

Emily's hair and she styled mine and then we both styled Lily's hair. I did one side and Emily did the other, plaiting it carefully and arranging her daisy slides. Lily wasn't too sure about this at first but then she got into the swing of it and said, 'Ur ur ur ur ur,' very happily.

'Oh Lily, you look *lovely*!' said Mum, and she looked like she was going to cry.

'You look utterly gorgeous, little Lily,' said Dad, pretending to bow to her. He put his arm round Emily and me. 'And you two look ultra-fantastic too.'

Emily and I beamed. And then her mum came to collect her. Emily gave me a special big hug and said it had been the best sleepover ever, ever, ever. Then she paused.

'I'm going to break friends with Chloe, Daisy – somehow! So will you be my new best friend?'

'Oh yes *please*, Emily! I'd like that more than anything!' I said.

I was so-o-o-o-o-o happy. But I was also a tiny bit scared too, wondering what Chloe would say, worrying what Chloe would *do*.

But you'll never ever guess what! We didn't have to break friends with Chloe. She broke friends with *us*!

When I got to school on Monday morning Chloe was telling a whole gang of girls that she'd been to the worst sleepover party in the world on Saturday.

'Daisy's house is all little and poky and there's no room anywhere and she's got this totally batty, loopy, maniac baby sister who screams all the time.' Chloe screwed up her face into a mad leer and wailed. Some of the girls laughed. I clenched my fists.

'You shut up, Chloe. My sister isn't mad. She's got learning difficulties, that's all.'

'She isn't Daisy's baby sister, she's her big sister. I like her a lot,' said Emily.

'She's special because she's got special needs,' said Amy.

'It's sad because she can't do much but she can still eat chocolate,' said Bella.

'Why are you all sticking up for Daisy Diddums and her loopy baby sister?' said Chloe, scowling.

'They're not the babies. *You* are,' said Emily. Chloe paused. She went red. She realized we all knew about her little accident. She waited, wondering if we were actually going to come out with it in front of everyone.

We waited too.

'You're not my best friend any more, Emily. You're not my friends either, Amy and Bella. And I wouldn't have *you* for a friend if you were the last girl in the world, Daisy Diddums,' said Chloe, and she turned her back on us and went off with this new gang of girls.

It was so-o-o-o-o wonderful! So now Emily and I are best friends and Amy and Bella are best friends and we all go round in a special foursome at school. Chloe doesn't look as if she likes it but there's nothing she can do about it – she knows we could still tell on her.

It's all because of Lily! She's the best sister ever.

TRACY BEAKER'S THUMPING HEART

To Doctor Sion Gibby
Dr Arvind Vasudeva
Dr John Foran
and all the staff at
St Anthony's Hospital and
the Royal Brompton Hospital
who looked after my own
thumping heart.

☆ TRACY BEAKER'S ☆ THUMPING HEART

It all started on St Valentine's Day. I'd never bothered about February 14th before. I don't go in for all that lovey-dovey slop. I certainly don't go a bundle on those sentimental satin hearts and huggy teddies and fat pink Cupid babies with wings. I'm Tracy Beaker, OK? Enough said.

I live in a Dumping Ground. It's actually a Children's Home for looked-after kids. Ha. You only end up here if you're *not* looked after. It isn't a home at all. It's definitely a dump.

I'm only there on a temporary basis of course. My mum's coming for me soon, just you wait and see. I know she misses me every bit as much as I miss her. It's just that she's otherwise engaged, holed up in Hollywood, making movies. She really is. Justine-

Know-Nothing-Littlewood says I'm making it all up but you don't want to take any notice of *her*. I just have to flash my special photo of my mum and it's perfectly obvious she's a film star. She's got lovely blonde wavy hair and big blue eyes and shiny pink lips. She's the prettiest woman

I've ever seen in my life. Even Justine-Argy-Bargy-Littlewood doesn't dispute that.

'So how come she's got such an ugly little squirt for a daughter?' Justine said, jabbing at the photo, poking the baby Tracy right in the tummy. I'm in my mum's arms, cuddling up to her. I look cute as a button, all smiles, with tiny tufts on the top of my head. I'm not quite as cute nowadays. I generally glare rather than grin and my curls have exploded all over so that I resemble a fuzzy floor mop. However, I am still *much* better looking than Justine-Bulgy-Eyed-Bullfrog-Littlewood.

prod

I might not be a Raving Beauty but I have Character. People say this all the time. I once had a social worker who was forever calling me a Right Little Character.

Elaine the Pain

I'm not sure how my current social worker Elaine the Pain would refer to me. I would possibly have to Delete some Expletives. I have an amazing vocabulary and often use long words. Expletives are *rude* words. (I often use them too!)

I won't need a social worker when my mum puts in an appearance, obviously. I expect this will be VERY SOON, the moment she's finished her mega movie commitments. Those Hollywood moguls are certainly keeping her busy as she hasn't written to me for *ages*.

I've got Mike and Jenny, who work at the Dumping Ground, on red alert for any phone calls from my mum. I often ask if she's phoned. Every day. Sometimes two or three times. They always sigh and say, 'No, sorry, Tracy' in this exasperated way. Exasperated is a posh word. It means people getting fed up with me. Folk are frequently exasperated when they deal with me.

It's not *my* fault. If only they wouldn't be so mean and give me my own mobile then I could make my own phone calls, no problem. A mobile is a bare necessity of modern life, for goodness' sake. I think it's outrageous that none of us kids in the Dumping Ground are allowed one until we're officially teenage, and even then it's a bog-standard pay-as-you-go embarrassment. Even Adele is limited to this type of manky mobile, and she's the oldest and coolest girl in the Dumping Ground. She's going to get her own flat soon. She's forever making plans for how she's going to furnish it and what she's going to do there.

'It's going to be Party Time every night of the week!' she says.

I hope she invites me to her parties. Adele is my favourite at the Dumping Ground. We hang out together lots. OK, she gets a bit Exasperated – with a capital E – when I experiment with her make-up and try walking in her amazing high heels.

She has been known to say, 'Jolly well clear off, Tracy Blooming Beaker' – or expletive words to that effect.

She's only kidding. She totally appreciates my company. In fact she frequently begs me to be her best friend. I might capitulate. (*Very* posh word for give in.) I very very rarely capitulate. I am one tough cookie who knows her own mind.

I *used* to be best friends with Louise. She's the prettiest kid here, with big blue eyes and long fair curls. She's *almost* as pretty as my mum. She looks as sweet as sugar but she's actually as sharp as knives. We used to have such fun together until Justine-Poach-My-Pal-Littlewood came along and stole her away from me.

Of course I could always get Louise back again as my best friend, easy peasy. But she's lost her chance. I don't *want* her now.

Adele is much more fun. Lots of people think so too. This was *abundantly* obvious on Saturday morning, Valentine's Day . . .

We were all sitting having our breakfast at the long table in the kitchen. The little kids were all strapped into their highchairs at one end, waving their soggy rusks and spooning up their mashed banana.

Maxy was kept up that end too. He's big enough to sit on a bench with us but you need to keep *way* clear of him when he tucks into his cornflakes and slurps his orange juice. He doesn't just *spill*. He's such a greedy little beggar he gollops it all down too quickly, chokes, and then spurts it all out like a fountain – *not* a pretty sight.

The rest of us kids with passable table manners cluster together. I always used to sit beside Louise but now Justine-Jabbing-Elbows-Littlewood does her best to make me unwelcome. I generally sit next to Adele – and weedy Peter nudges up to my other side more often than not.

I haven't mentioned Peter up till now, though he actually plays an important part in this story. This is surprising because if you saw a photo of all of us kids in the Dumping Ground you'd find him the least significant. He's this weird little geeky kid with big eyes like Bambi and arms and legs as spindly as spaghetti.

He's always clutching a soggy lacy hankie in his little paw. It used to belong to his nan who looked after him until she died and little Pete got dumped alongside us. He hangs on to it like it's his cuddle blanket. It's soggy because he's frequently in tears. He's much too old for all his namby-pamby snuffles. He might only look about six but he's my age. *Exactly* my age. He has the cheek to have the same birthday as me so we have to share a birthday cake between us. We might share our star sign but we have NOTHING in common.

I never cry. I didn't even cry when Louise went off with Justine and they stole my totally private diary and wrote ludicrous lies all over it. I didn't so much as whimper when my mum forgot to send me a present last birthday. Correction: of course she sent me a present. Loads of them. A karaoke kit for definite. And maybe my own mobile, and a little laptop and an iPod and a genuine cowboy hat and new football boots, all sorts of stuff, but they somehow got lost in the post, stolen before I could lay my hands on my parcels. But I *still* didn't cry. I might have the odd attack of hayfever which everyone knows makes your eyes stream – but I never cry.

'I know you don't ever cry, Tracy,' says Peter. 'You are *soooo* brave.'

He isn't taking the micky. He idolizes me. This is somewhat irritating. He trots round after me and hangs on my every word, no matter what. I don't *want* him acting like my little shadow. I frequently tell him to shove off. But then his little white face crumples up and he has to mop his big eyes with his Nanny rag. This is an infuriating ploy. It makes you feel mean and then you have to be sweet to him to stop him blabbing. I'll offer him a bite of my Mars bar or I'll teach him a new naughty word or if I'm *really* feeling kind I'll tickle him under his scrawny little arms. He'll nibble at the Mars and gasp at the rude word and squeal when he's tickled and tell me that I'm the best kid in the Dumping Ground. In our town, in our county, in our country, in our world, in our own ultra-extensive universe.

I just nod and go, 'Yeah yeah yeah' because I know this already. I'm Tracy Beaker, right?

So Peter was sitting next to me at breakfast on the fourteenth. He nudged up so close he was practically sitting in my lap.

'Give us a bit of elbow room, Peter,' I said, giving him a shove.

'Sorry, Tracy,' he said, but he wriggled even closer so that his mouth was right next to my ear. 'I want to ask you something,' he said, his whisper tickling terribly inside my ear.

'What?' I said loudly, rubbing my ear.

'Sh! It's a secret,' said Peter.

I sighed. Peter was forever telling me secrets

and they weren't very exciting. He'd confide enormously embarrassing stuff, like he sometimes wet the bed at night, as if he imagined this wasn't obvious to everyone, seeing as he wandered round the Home half the night trailing damp sheets like a waterlogged ghost.

'Tracy, it's the fourteenth of February today,' Peter whispered.

'That's not a secret,' I said.

'It's Valentine's Day,' Peter persisted.

'That's not a secret *either*,' I said, exasperated.

'Tracy, will you be my Valentine sweetheart?' Peter whispered.

'What? Oh yuck, Pete, I don't believe in all that sentimental slush,' I said.

'*I* do,' said Peter. 'Oh, Tracy, please say you will.'

He blinked at me with his big Bambi eyes. Justine-Big-Nose-Littlewood was peering in our direction, looking inquisitive.

'OK, but shut up about it now, right?' I hissed.

'So that's a yes?' said Peter, kicking his legs jubilantly under the table. He just happened quite by wondrous chance to kick Justine-Daddy-Long-Legs-Littlewood right in the shins!

'Ouch!' Justine shrieked.

'Well *done*, Peter,' I said. I gave him such a congratulatory clap on the back he nearly shot across the table top. Maxy stopped slurping cornflakes and shrieked with delight. He choked, with predictable results.

'Simmer down, kids,' said Jenny. 'This is worse than feeding time at the zoo.'

'Yeah, yeah, me a wild animal,' said Maxy, scratching himself vigorously and snatching a plate of mashed banana from one of the babies, who started howling.

Rat-a-tat-tat!

'Behave, you lot!' said Mike, wielding his big wooden spoon, pretending to rap all our knuckles.

There was another rap at the front door, an important official rat-a-tat-tat. I felt a familiar clutch at my chest. I always wondered if it could possibly be my mum come calling for me at long last. All the noise of the room faded and I just heard the thump thump thump of my heart. Then Jenny came back into the kitchen with a huge pile of post in her arms.

'It was the postie,' she said. 'Hey guys, Valentine's cards!'

The babies went on spooning their banana, Maxy elaborated on his animal imitation, but the rest of us sat upright, twitching. I suddenly *got* it. It was a competition. Who was going to get the most Valentine's cards???

Jenny was sorting through them all, giggling, especially when she found a card addressed to herself. Mike had a card as well, a big funny one that played a silly tune when he opened it up.

I stared at the rest of the cards in Jenny's hands. She doled them out. One for Justine-Absolutely-Ugly-Littlewood!!! Who on *earth* would send a Valentine's card to her?

She seemed thrilled with it too, reading the dumb verse over and over and stroking the glittering silver heart on the front.

'Who's it *from*, Justine?' Louise asked. 'I didn't know you had a boyfriend! What's his *name*? Look, he's signed it!'

'I'm not telling. It's a secret,' said Justine-Smug-Git-Littlewood, clapping her card to her chest.

'You haven't got a boyfriend, not unless he's blind and stupid,' I said fiercely. 'I bet you sent that card to yourself!'

'No, I didn't, Sour-Grapes-Nobody-Loves-You-Beaker,' said Justine-Smug-Bug-Littlewood.

'Take no notice, Tracy,' Peter whispered right in my ear. 'She's talking rubbish. *I* love you. I'll make you a special Valentine's card.'

I couldn't concentrate on Peter and his tickly whisper and his offer of a crayoned card. I reached right over the table and snatched Justine's card. I only saw it for a second before she snatched it back, acting outraged, but it was enough time to read the message and the signature. It wasn't from a boyfriend at all. The card said *To dear Justine, Happy Valentine's Day, Love from Dad.*

I felt as if I'd been stabbed in the stomach. It was much much better than a card from a stupid boyfriend. I didn't even *have* a dad. Not that I cared. I had a mum and she was all that mattered to me. Had *she* sent me a Valentine's card?

I waited while Jenny went on dealing them all out. Louise got one. Louise got another. Louise got *three*! They were all from boys at school. They were all nuts about her.

She kept giggling, pink in the face, *sooo* pleased.

'Hey, Louise has got *three* Valentines, look!' crowed Justine-Brag-A-Lot-Littlewood. 'Louise has got more Valentines than anyone else. So that proves she's the most popular girl here.'

'Not absolutely accurate,' said Adele, as Jenny gave her a *handful* of cards, one, two, three, four, *five* Valentines. The last was a huge one with a big red satin heart and a badge saying *Happy Valentine, Love you Lots, Babe*. Adele chuckled and pinned it on her top.

'Adele's got *five* Valentines, way more than anyone else in the whole Dumping Ground,' I said. 'So *she's* the most popular girl, right?'

'Adele doesn't properly count. She's not really a girl, she's nearly grown up, and she's got heaps of boyfriends anyway,' said Justine-Pedant-Littlewood. 'Louise got the most Valentines of all us kids. And I've got the prettiest Valentine because of all the silver glitter and the lovely verse. What have you got, Tracy Beaker? Absolute *zilch*.'

'That's all *you* know, Justine-Rubbish-Littlewood,' I said.

Jenny still had a few cards left. Maybe maybe maybe one was for *me*. If Justine's dad had sent her a card maybe my mum *might* just have decided to send me a Valentine. It would be a cool way for her to keep in touch. Maybe she'd write a special message: *To my darling little Tracy, Happy Valentine's Day, See you Very Soon, Lots of love, Mum*.

Jenny kept handing out the cards. She held up the last one, giggling, because it was another one addressed to *her*.

'Don't look so desperate, Tracy Beaker. Look, she's nearly in tears. Boo-hoo baby. Fancy getting in such a stupid state. No one would ever dream of sending *you* a Valentine,' said Justine Asking-For-A-Punch-Littlewood.

'That's just where you're wrong,' I said. I spoke slightly indistinctly. 'Absolutely one hundred percent wrong,' said Peter. 'I happen to know Tracy will be getting an enormous and very special card as soon as possible.'

'We don't count scribbly home-made efforts from little weeds,' said Justine-Crushing-Littlewood.

'She's not just getting a card, she's getting a Valentine's *present*!' Peter declared. 'She's getting it right this minute. Just you wait till you see what it is.'

He jumped off the bench and ran out of the room. Justine and Louise tittered together, while Mike went, 'Aaaah!' and Jenny went, 'Sweet!'

'I bet that's what he's going to give her – a sweet,' said Justine-Scoffing-Littlewood. 'He'll have probably sucked it first!'

Peter came charging back, carrying *something* in a tremendously sellotaped brown paper bag. He thrust it at me triumphantly. Oh dear, oh dear, oh dear. What on earth would it be? A marble? A ten pence piece? A pebble with a message scratched in biro?

I knew just how much Justine would jeer.

'I think I'll open my parcel in private,' I said, simply trying to save Peter's feelings.

'No, no, open it *now*,' said Peter. 'You wait and see, Justine. Tracy's got a *fabulous* Valentine's present.'

'So you're giving her a Valentine's present, are you, little Petey-Wetey-Wet-The-Bed. Ah, how touching!' said Justine-Viper-Tongue-Littlewood.

Peter's white face flushed raspberry red.

'I *don't* wet the bed, Justine. And anyway, even if I did, Jenny says it's nothing at all to be ashamed of,' said Peter.

'Absolutely spot on, Peter,' said Jenny, her nose still inside her Valentine's cards. 'Come on, Tracy, open your present. We're all dying to see what it is.'

I could see there was absolutely no way I could sneak off and open Peter's wretched parcel in private. I decided to brazen it out. If Justine dared sneer I'd pick up Maxy, shoogle him violently up and down and then aim him in her direction.

I struggled with my bitten nails to prise back the sellotape. It looked as if I might need bolt-cutters. I improvised, biting my way in. I peeled back layers of crumpled tissues – and stared at Peter's Valentine's present.

'What is it, then? Let us see!' said Justine-Long-Nosed-Littlewood.

I silently held it up. It was a beautiful gold locket in the shape of a heart. Real gold. The heart was huge, almost as big as my fist. A gold heart like that must be worth hundreds and hundreds of pounds! Everyone gasped.

'Where on earth did you get *that*, Peter? You didn't nick it, did you?' said Louise.

'Don't be ridiculous, Louise,' said Jenny. She looked astounded too. 'Where *did* you get the locket from, Peter?' she asked.

'I've kept it hidden in a sock ever since I came here. It was my nan's,' said Peter. He said it proudly but his eyes filled with tears. He nearly always cried when he talked about his nan. 'She used to wear it on Sundays. It had a chain to match but I'm afraid it got broken. But the locket's still fine. Look, Tracy, you just press this little catch, see.'

He demonstrated with his small finger and the locket opened. There was a photo of an infant inside, a pale baby with little downy curls, big Bambi eyes, sticking out ears and a very skinny neck.

'That's me,' Peter said unnecessarily. He edged up to me again, whispering so the others wouldn't hear. 'Nan used to say I was her little sweetheart. Now I'm your Valentine sweetheart, aren't I, Tracy?'

I didn't know what to say. I remembered the time Mike and Jenny took all us kids to a theme park and I went on the rollercoaster. My stomach felt exactly the same now. I was touched that weedy little Peter liked me enough to give me his nan's incredibly valuable locket – but all that sentimental sweetheart stuff made me want to throw up.

'What do you *say*, Tracy?' Mike prompted me.

I still couldn't speak. I held the gold locket tight in my hand and stared hard at the table top, praying that I wasn't about to succumb to an inconvenient bout of hayfever.

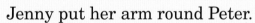

Jenny put her arm round Peter.

'It's such a sweet romantic gesture, Peter, but are you really sure you want to give your nan's very special heart to Tracy?'

'Of course he's sure!' I said indignantly.

'Maybe you could give Tracy the heart just for today?' Jenny persisted.

'What kind of a rum deal is that?' I said. 'Presents are meant to be *permanent*.'

'I want to give Tracy the heart for ever and ever,' said Peter fervently.

Justine-Has-To-Mock-Littlewood made silly whistling noises, rolling her eyes. Louise and the other kids copied her – but Adele smiled.

'Aah, you're such a little gent, Pete,' she said. 'You're a very lucky girl, Tracy.'

I nodded, clutching my gold heart.

'Now you'll have to find a very special place to keep your heart, Tracy,' said Jenny. 'It must be *very* valuable. I think I'd better pop it in the safe for the moment.'

'No way! I'm wearing it!' I said.

'For goodness' sake, Tracy, you're the girl who's always losing everything,' said Jenny. 'This week it was your pen, last week your swimming kit – and didn't we have to fork out for an entire new school bag for you last month? Of course I can't let you wear a real gold locket. Anyway, you haven't got a chain.'

'I'll *make* a special chain. Oh, Jenny, please, it means so much to me. No one's ever given me such a special incredibly expensive present – apart from my mum, of course,' I said, laying it on thick.

'Go on, Jenny, let her wear her locket!' said Mike.

'All right. You can wear it at the weekends, Tracy, so long as you look after it ultra-carefully. I haven't got the heart to argue with you any more. *Heart*, get it!'

I tittered obligingly and sauntered off to manufacture my chain. Peter skipped along beside me, beaming so brightly his lips nearly met at the back of his head.

'Do you really really really like your Valentine's locket, Tracy?' he burbled.

'Yes, I do. I'm going to wear it all the time, even at school. I'll get round Jenny somehow. I can't wait to show it off. It's so big! It must be worth a fortune!'

'Well, to be absolutely truthful it isn't really worth a fortune, Tracy. It isn't actually *gold* gold,' said Peter, looking very worried.

'What are you on about? Of *course* it's gold,' I said, holding the locket up.

'It's just gold-*coloured*, Tracy. My granddad won it for my nan at a fairground. You have to keep polishing it like crazy or it goes a sort of green colour – but I've made it lovely and shiny now. It *looks* like real gold. You don't mind that it isn't *actually* gold, do you, Tracy?'

I minded terribly. I'd never owned any real jewellery before. None of the kids in the Dumping Ground had *proper* jewellery. Adele had sparkly studs in her ears but they weren't real diamonds. Justine-Tacky-Littlewood and Louise just had yucky bead friendship bracelets.

I so wanted everyone to envy me having a real gold heart locket worth a fortune. They'd all laugh at me if they knew it was a trashy old fairground prize. I couldn't let them find out.

'To me it's real gold, Peter,' I said firmly, threading it on a piece of string.

It didn't have exactly the right effect. I sidled into Adele's room while she was in the bathroom and had a quick rummage through her dressing-table drawers. I came across just the job, a white broderie anglaise blouse threaded with thin red velvet ribbon. I wondered about asking . . . but Adele was still a bit narked because I'd dressed up in her black high heels to be a Spanish dancer and I'd stamped a little too vigorously and one of the silly heels fell off. She'd said I couldn't ever ever ever borrow her clothes again.

Oops!

I didn't want to borrow her whole blouse, just the red velvet ribbon running round it, but I still had a funny feeling she'd object. So I had one quick tug at the ribbon and suddenly there it was, in my hand. I charged back to my room and tied it with the gold heart. It looked great! Oh dear, if only it were *real* solid gold and worth something!

'It looks lovely on you, Tracy,' said Peter.

'Yes, it does,' I said, smoothing the ribbon and stroking the heart.

'So we're really sweethearts now?' Peter said eagerly.

'If you say so,' I said.

'Oh, I do! I really love you, Tracy.'

He waited, his head on one side.

'Do you love me, Tracy?'

'Oh, *Pete*. Look, I'm not into all that dopey lovey-dovey stuff.'

He blinked his big Bambi eyes, his lip starting to tremble.

'Don't look so *stricken*! It's not *you*, Peter. It's not personal at all. I'm never going to fall in love. I'm Tracy Beaker. I'm *immune*.'

Little did I know that sneaky baby Cupid was lurking in a corner, arrow poised, about to pierce my heart.

I did a little tap dance downstairs, my gold heart bouncing on the end of the red ribbon. I paused at the window on the landing. You could see all the way down the drive to the gates at the end. I usually leaned against this window and waited on Saturdays. I paused here today.

'Are you watching out for . . . anyone?' Peter asked delicately.

I nodded.

'I'll wait with you,' said Peter.

He didn't have anyone to watch for, not unless his own nan popped down a celestial ladder from heaven and shuffled up the drive in her Dr Scholl's. He was just keeping me company.

I was watching for my mum of course. She's going to come and see me very soon. I might just have mentioned this before. Justine-Relentlessly-Evil-Littlewood says my mum's forgotten all about me and isn't ever going to come and see me. But she is *sooo* wrong and if she says it again I'll punch her on the nose. Of course my mum's coming. Very very soon. On Saturday. That's what she said when I last saw her.

It was quite a long time ago but I remember every single second so very clearly. Mum took me out and we went for this incredibly posh meal. I couldn't *believe* the prices! It meant my mum thought the whole world of me. She let me order absolutely everything I fancied on the menu, with a double portion of French fries and then *two* puddings and *then* lots of little chocolates on a pretty saucer.

It was the best meal I'd ever had. I didn't hang on to it for very long. I was so excited to see my mum that my tummy went fizz fizz fizz and I had to gallop in double-quick time to the ladies' where I was horribly sick. Mum was a bit cross with me then and I don't blame her because she'd forked out a small fortune on that meal then I'd wasted it all. But she mopped me up and we went to buy me a new top because the one I was wearing got a bit splashed.

It wasn't just an ordinary T-shirt from Primark – it was *designer*. Mum didn't flinch as she flashed her credit card.

Then Mum took me to the cinema. I so hoped it was going to be one of Mum's films and I'd see her acting at last, but it was a cartoon film. It had a fairy-tale princess in it, with long golden hair just like my mum though. And then Mum took me back to the Dumping Ground and I had a very severe attack of hayfever.

Mum told me I mustn't make such a silly fuss, she'd come and get me for good as soon as she could get everything sorted, and meanwhile she'd visit me as often as possible.

'Next Saturday?' I said, and Mum said, 'Sure.' She even called, 'See you Saturday' as she waved and went down the drive.

So I waited. I thought she meant the actual *next* Saturday but she didn't come. Then I realized she meant *a* Saturday. So I wait for her every Saturday, watching from the window to get the first glimpse of her. I stand at the window and stare out, concentrating hard. I stare at the gates and will Mum to walk through them.

So I stared and stared and stared, and Peter stood beside me, staring too. Then I heard Adele shouting that *someone* had been in her room messing about with her clothes, and I felt a little too prominent in my window-watching position. I scooted downstairs, Peter at my side, and went into our sitting room. Maxy was watching television while still eating his breakfast toast. He was so absorbed watching some silly cartoon that he frequently missed his mouth, smearing butter all over his cheeks and chin.

'Tracy's my Valentine sweetheart,' Peter said.

Maxy grunted, unimpressed.

'I think you should be Justine's sweetheart, Maxy. The minute she comes downstairs run and give her a great big kiss. Rub your face all over her,' I said.

'Really?' Maxy said indistinctly.

'Absolutely,' I said, although Peter frowned at me.

'*Swap Shop*'s starting on the other channel,' said Peter. 'Let's watch that instead. It's good, isn't it, Tracy?'

I shrugged. I didn't know any of the Saturday morning shows because of my weekly vigil on the stairs, but I'd heard some of the other kids talking about it. There was this funny furry little fox telling silly jokes, and there was some young guy presenter, Billy or Barry or . . . 'Hi, I'm Barney.'

He was smiling straight out of the television – straight at *me*. His warm brown eyes shone and his cheeky face lit up. I loved his funny monkey T-shirt. He looked like a big brother who loved fooling around and making jokes – and yet he had big strong arms that could give you a hug, just like a dad.

There was a *twang* in the room as that pesky little Cupid shot his arrow, and a *thunk* as it shot straight through my sweater and pierced my heart. Not Peter's nan's not-real-gold locket. My own red thumping heart pulsing inside my ribcage.

I sat down beside Maxy, even though I was risking getting a piece of chewed toast stuck in my ear. Peter sat neatly cross-legged on the other side of me.

'This is a good programme, Tracy,' he said. 'I love Basil Brush. And I like Barney too. Do you like him?'

'Yeah, he's OK,' I mumbled. Like! He was *fantastic*!

Barney smiled as if he could hear us.

'Who likes a hearty breakfast?' he asked, grinning. 'Cupid!'

I snorted with laughter.

'Did you get any Valentine cards today?' asked Barney. 'I didn't, sob sob.'

'I got hundreds!' said Basil Brush. 'I know a lot of foxy ladies – boom boom!'

Barney sighed and rolled his brown eyes. 'Here's a little Valentine verse just for you.'

He was looking straight at me!

'Roses are red,

Violets are blue,

Watch *Swap Shop* on Saturday

And I'll love you true.'

'I'll love *you*, Barney,' I said inside my head.

He nodded and gave me a wink. But our thrilling telepathy was suddenly obliterated by Justine-Foghorn-Littlewood barging into the room, shrieking with laughter over something stupid. Maxy hurled himself at her and nuzzled her neck romantically. He spread slime, snot and soggy toast all over her head, hair and sweater in a highly satisfactory fashion. She shrieked even louder.

Mike came running, convinced she was being murdered (I *wish*!). When he'd calmed her down he stayed to watch *Swap Shop* with us.

'I used to watch *Swap Shop* when *I* was a kid,' he said. 'And is that Basil Brush? He doesn't look quite the same. I'm sure his snout used to be more pointy. He looks a bit too cuddly now. Who's the scruffy guy with him? He used to be with Mr Derek.'

'Oh Mike, you are hopeless! That's Barney. Justine and I think he's seriously cool,' said Louise.

How dare they! He was *my* Barney!

'Yeah, we like his funky little bit of face-fuzz,' said Justine-Leery-Eyes-Littlewood, mopping herself with a J-cloth. 'Hey look, that girl wants to swap a karaoke kit for something else. Is she *mad*? I'd give anything for one. I'm going to phone in and offer to swap it for . . . What can I offer, Lou?'

'I could offer my hair-straightening kit now I've decided to go for the naturally curly look,' she said.

'I could swap my rubber Dumbo for it,' said Maxy.

'*You're* the Dumbo, Maxy! It's worth about five pence maximum after you've slobbered all over it,' said Justine-Spurn-Her-Sweetheart-Littlewood. 'You've got to swap something of equivalent value. A karaoke kit is worth *heaps*.'

'Do you want a karaoke kit, Tracy?' Peter said.

Of *course* I did. It would be so cool to plug it in and belt out a little number with proper musical accompaniment. Maybe I could even croon a ballad for Barney! Only what could I swap? My possessions were as manky as Maxy's. All my books were wrinkly because I read them in the bath. My skateboard buckled that time I played dodgem dustbins. My CD player broke when I dropped it down the stairs. I'd lost my left flashing trainer and my right footie boot and *both* my rollerblades. I didn't have anything – and yet I *so* wanted a karaoke machine.

I was sure I could sing better than the stars. It would be my chance to be discovered. Forget Amy, forget Lily. You're toast, Rihanna and Duffy. Tracy Beaker, singing superstar, is taking to the stage.

My heart started thumping. I fingered my gold heart locket. It wasn't real gold but it looked like it. Jenny and Mike and all the other kids except Peter thought it was real gold and worth a fortune. Worth way more than a karaoke machine. But I couldn't swap Peter's heart . . . could I?

It wasn't Peter's any more though. He'd given it to me. I could legitimately do what I liked with it: keep it in my treasure box, wear it on a ribbon, sell it to a jeweller, *swap it* . . . And it wasn't as if it was *worth* anything.

Justine-Out-To-Outdo-Me-Littlewood was already begging Mike to lend her his mobile.

'Quick, quick, I need to get through to *Swap Shop now*, Mike. Louise and I are offering to swap her hair-straightening kit.'

'Are you OK with this, Louise?' said Mike. 'It's *your* hair-straightening do-da.'

'Yes, that's fine. Justine and I will share the karaoke machine,' said Louise.

'That's what best friends are for. Sharing!' said Justine-Snatch-*My*-Friend-Littlewood.

I felt as if she'd punched me in the chest. My heart thumped. I suddenly put my arm round Peter. *'We're* best friends, aren't we, Pete?' I said.

'Oh *yes*, Tracy,' said Peter, his big eyes shining. 'Sweethearts *and* best friends.'

'We'd like to share a karaoke kit, wouldn't we?' I said.

Peter nodded a little less certainly.

'If only we had something brilliant to swap,' I said. 'Something worth much much more than a silly old hair-straightening kit. Can you think of anything, Peter?'

Peter blinked, looking bewildered.

'Quick, quick, Justine's phoning already. We *have* to outbid her!' I said urgently. 'Think, Pete, think! Have we got *anything*?'

I fingered the heart locket ostentatiously (meaning I practically thrust it in Peter's face). He gazed at it, a little cross-eyed.

'Well . . . all I can think of is my nan's heart locket,' he said.

'Yes! Yes, of course! Oh well done, Peter! You're sure you don't mind?' I gabbled, pulling him over towards Mike.

'Well, it's your heart locket now, Tracy. Don't *you* mind?' said Peter.

'Of course I mind. Very much,' I said. 'But we both know it isn't really worth anything. And it looks pretty but it doesn't really *do* anything, does it? Not like a karaoke machine. I'll let you have first go if we can swap it.'

'Hey, Tracy, what are you talking about?' said Mike. 'What are you saying to Peter? You're not saying you want to swap his nan's *heart*?'

'It's OK, it's not *real* gold, so it's not like it's really valuable – only *they're* not to know,' I hissed, and I grabbed the phone from Justine-Long-Winded-Littlewood.

'Give that back, I haven't finished!' she shrieked.

'You've *had* your turn. It's *mine* now,' I insisted. 'Isn't that right, Pete?'

'Hey hey hey!' said the guy at the end of the phone. 'Stop squabbling, you lot!'

'Is that *you*, Barney?' I said, hanging onto the phone, fingers superglued to the handset.

'No, sorry, I'm not Barney. Or Basil Brush either.'

'Boom boom!' I said.

'Exactly,' said the person. 'I'm Ben. I just work for the programme. Now, are you all one family? I've got Justine's name down – and Louise too. Are they your sisters?'

'NO WAY!' I said. 'Take no notice of their pathetic offering. Whoever wants a boring old hair-straightening kit?'

'You certainly *need* one, Tracy Beaker. You look like your head's been plugged into a light socket,' yelled Justine-Big-Gob-Littlewood.

'Shut *up*, Justine,' I bellowed. 'This is my turn. Isn't it, Ben?' I said down the telephone.

'If you say so,' said Ben.

'I want to talk too!' said Maxy, grabbing for the phone with his revoltingly sticky paws.

'No, get *off*, Maxy! Yuck, you're getting slurp all over my skirt, stop it!'

'Are you watching *Swap Shop* with a whole bunch of friends?' said Ben.

'Do we *sound* like friends?' I asked, mega-exasperated. 'More like deadly enemies! We live in this Dumping Ground.'

'Tracy!' said Mike. 'Children's Home, *if* you please. And hurry up, that's my own personal phone and you're costing me a fortune.'

'I'm *trying* to hurry up,' I said. 'Listen, Ben, I've got this amazing gold locket. I just *know* that karaoke girl will want to swap for it.'

'Are you sure it's *your* gold heart locket, Tracy?' asked Ben. 'It's not your mum's?'

'Of course it's not my *mum's*. As if I'd want to swap it then!' I said. 'No, it's a long story. My friend Peter gave it to me, for Valentine's day, actually, but we both think a karaoke set would be *way* more exciting, don't we, Peter?'

I prodded him and he nodded, though his bottom lip was quivering for some reason.

'Well, if there's an interesting story attached to this heart maybe you and some of your friends – or deadly enemies – might like to come along to the *Swap Shop* studio next week. You could show off your gold locket, Tracy.'

'And I'll meet Barney?'

'You'll meet everyone – Melvyn, Basil Brush, Frosty the Snowman, Keith the swapping hamster – *and* Barney. I think it would be a great idea for all you guys to be in our skip full of kids. You and Peter and Justine and Louise and Maxy and any other of your pals in the Children's Home. You could try to swap a karaoke set for all of you. Tracy, you've gone very quiet. You're still there, aren't you?'

'Yes,' I said. 'Um, can you just run that past me again, Ben? You're saying I'm invited to the studio to meet Barney, and I'm going to be, like, on *television*? Me, Tracy Beaker?'

'*What*?' shrieked Justine-Totally-Jealous-Littlewood. 'Tracy Beaker's going to be on *Swap Shop*? That's not FAIR! It was all *my* idea. I phoned up first. *I* should be picked to go on television!'

'Pipe down, you lot!' Mike bellowed. 'Would you mind handing me my phone, please? If *any* of you are appearing on television then *I* need to be involved. Shh, the lot of you!'

He talked long and earnestly, sometimes nodding, sometimes shaking his head, while we listened, holding our breath.

'Well, thank you so much. I'll email you all the details,' said Mike, and he switched off his phone.

We all started clamouring. He held up his arms for silence.

'OK kids, they want six of you there at the studios next week for the show. It's all fixed.'

'HURRAY! HURRAY! HURRAY!' we shrieked, jumping up and down.

Justine-Still-Not-My-Friend-Littlewood hugged Louise. I was so jubilant I hugged Maxy, rendering myself seriously sticky, in need of a thorough hosing down. I went to hug Peter too but he hung back, rubbing his cuddle hankie against his nose.

'What's up, Peter? Come on, be *happy*, we're going to be on television!' I said, giving him a little shake.

'I'm not sure I *want* to be on television,' he said in a tiny voice, muffled behind his hankie.

'Of course you do. Don't worry, you don't have to *say* anything. I'll say it all for you.'

'Yeah, Tracy-Big-Blabbermouth,' said Justine-She-Can-Talk-Littlewood.

'You can just shut up, Justine. I don't know why *you're* jumping up and down like a jackass because *you're* not going. Or you, Louise. *I'm* the one they invited. Me, Tracy Beaker. *I* get to choose my five companions. Get it?'

'Stop shouting, Tracy,' said Jenny, coming in from the kitchen with a baby on either hip. 'What were you all yelling about? What's going on, Mike?'

'The kids are going to be on *Swap Shop* on the telly next week,' said Mike, grinning.

'Oh no they're not,' said Jenny.

'Oh yes we *are*,' I said, sounding like we were doing a pantomime routine.

'No, Tracy. I'm sorry, you *can't* be on television. There are all sorts of regulations about looked-after children. We'd never get permission in time,' said Jenny.

'Look, my mum's quite probably coming to see me this very Saturday so we can get her permission today,' I said.

'Now, Tracy, I know you'd love to see your mum, but you know she isn't really coming,' Jenny said very quietly.

'Yes, she is so!'

'Tracy, we're not even very sure where she *is* at the moment,' said Jenny.

'She's in Hollywood, I keep *telling* you! Are you deaf or stupid?' I yelled, hating Jenny.

'Ha ha ha, Tracy Beaker. *You* can't go but *I* can, because I see my dad heaps and he'd be over the moon to watch me on television,' crowed Justine-Impossibly-Hateful-Littlewood.

'No, you're not any of you going. It's against the rules and would involve endless paperwork,' said Jenny.

'Look, I've said they can go and they're *going*,' said Mike. 'Any other kid in the country can go on telly so why can't they? I don't care if it gets us into trouble. I'm taking them and that's that.'

We all fell on Mike, giving him huge hugs.

But it was Jenny who battled with all the phone calls and paperwork. I passed by her office and saw her simultaneously typing an email, talking on the phone and jiggling a whimpering baby on her lap. The baby kept trying to hurl herself onto her head just to add to Jenny's problems.

'That baby thinks she's a lemming,' I said.

'Here, I'll take her, shall I?'

I scooped the baby up. She blinked at me in surprise and then reached eagerly for the gold heart round my neck.

'Naughty! I don't want your tiny teeth-marks all over it. It's my special swap for Saturday,' I said.

Jenny snorted and muttered a very rude word about *Swap Shop*.

'Um! I wouldn't half get told off if *I* said that. Jenny, I *can* go on *Swap Shop*, can't I? I can't miss this huge big chance to star on television. I might get discovered, impress them so much they offer me my own kid's show. After all, acting's in my blood! Look at my mum, the famous Hollywood movie star.'

'Oh, Tracy,' said Jenny.

'She *is*,' I said. 'Just you wait, she'll be coming for me any day now.'

Jenny nodded wearily.

I waited, joggling the baby.

'Jenny . . .'

'Yes, Tracy.'

'You said you don't know where my mum is.'

'Mm.' Jenny reached out and stroked my arm. 'We've been trying to get in touch. Apparently she's moved on from her last known address.'

'Because she's in Hollywood. *Obviously*,' I said.

We looked at each other.

'Right,' said Jenny, sighing.

'Hey, hey, I told you no biting!' I said to the baby, who was drooling all over the heart.

'Tracy, about Peter's nan's locket—'

'It's *my* locket now.'

'Yes I know. But I don't think you realize that it's maybe very upsetting for Peter that you want to swap it straight away.'

'But it's not real gold. It's not worth anything, Jenny, I promise.'

'What about sentimental value?'

'You're talking to me, Tracy Beaker. I'm not into sentiment, Jenny,' I said briskly.

I did pursue the matter a little further with Peter though. I cornered him that night when we both had occasion to go to the linen cupboard for clean sheets.

'You're sure you're OK about me swapping my heart locket, Peter?' I said.

'Yes, that's fine, Tracy,' he said, snuffling into his nanny hankie.

 'It'll be *sooo* great to have a karaoke machine, won't it?' I said. 'We'll sing a duet, you and me, Peter. That will be fun, won't it?'

'Yes, Tracy,' Peter mumbled.

I gently unhooked his hankie from his nose and prodded the corners of his mouth.

'Smile, then!'

He smiled obediently. So that was all right then.

He wasn't smiling early on Saturday morning. He was crying.

'Oh, for goodness' sake, Pete, what's *up* with you? This is our big day,' I said, giving him a little shake.

'I've-lost-my-hankie!' he sobbed.

'What? Oh, give me a break! Get a tissue from the bathroom.'

'No, it's my nan's hankie, it got mixed up in the sheets and they're all higgledy-piggledy in the laundry basket and I can't *find* it!' Peter wailed.

'I'm not sure I'd *want* to find it in amongst a load of damp smelly sheets!' I said. 'Oh, cheer up, Peter. I'm sure Jenny will find it for you, and if she doesn't she'll get you a brand new hankie.'

'I don't want a new hankie, I want my *old* hankie that belonged to my nan,' Peter wept.

'Now look! This is our big day. It means *sooo* much to me. I'm going to meet Barney and get a karaoke machine! So don't spoil it for me, OK?' I said.

Peter blinked at me, sniffling. 'I'm sorry, Tracy,' he squeaked. He tried to smile again, even though the tears were still streaming down his cheeks.

'You are such a *baby*, Peter,' said Justine-Utterly-Lacking-Compassion-Littlewood. 'Hey, Lou, do you think I look OK in this top or should I change it?'

'It's lovely, keep it on. But what about me?' said Louise. 'I'm not sure about wearing pink. Is it, like, *too* girly?'

'Excuse me!' I said. 'As if it matters. No one will be looking at you. *I'm* the one doing the swap. You'll just be in the background, *lurking*.'

'Pulling faces behind you,' said Justine-Can't-Ever-Be-Trusted-Littlewood.

'I can pull really scary faces, look,' said Maxy, pulling his eyelids down and his nose up, grinning like a gargoyle.

'You're seriously scary all the time, Maxy,' said Mike, pretending to cower away from him. 'Right, you guys, are we ready for the off? One, two, three, four, five . . . Where's Adele? Adele, come on!'

'I'll get her,' I said, charging up the stairs.

Melvyn

I was worried she'd changed her mind. She'd said she didn't want to go on a silly little kids' programme, thank you very much – but she gave into my pleading when she caught a glimpse of Barney's pal Melvyn on the television.

'He looks kind of cute,' she'd said. 'I love the way he does his hair. OK, Tracy, if it means all that much to you I'll come. *If* I feel like it on the day.'

'Adele, Adele, *please* feel like coming! You're my best friend. You jolly well have to support me,' I said now, barging into her room.

'Hey, hey, I'm just putting on my make-up,' said Adele.

She looked incredible: amazing outlined eyes, pearly lips, glitter on her cheeks, just like a fashion model.

'Oh, wow, you look wonderful. Can *I* have some make-up too, Adele? Please please please make me up to look like you,' I begged, although I was conscious of Mike downstairs bellowing at us to get a move on.

'You're not old enough for proper make-up, Tracy,' said Adele.

'Just a speck of lippy,' I pleaded.

'You're lippy enough already,' said Adele. 'How about a splodge of red lipstick on your nose – the comic clown effect? It'll match your red velvet ribbon round your neck!' She scribbled scarlet on my nose. I shrieked – but she took her tissue and wiped it straight *off*.

'Come on, then, Tracy. You look fine just as you are, I promise,' said Adele, ruffling my corkscrew curls. She was staring at my customized locket chain. 'Why does that ribbon look weirdly familiar?'

I shrugged and rushed her downstairs hurriedly. Jenny and all the littlies waved us goodbye and wished us luck. We all climbed into the mini van and we were off.

There was a five minute squabble about who was sitting where,

everyone trying to steer well clear of Maxy, though Jenny had attacked him with an entire packet of wet wipes. Mike distracted us with a sing-song, and most of us joined in, practising for when I had my karaoke kit. Peter didn't sing very loudly. His voice was just a little mouse squeak.

As we got nearer and nearer the studio I found my tummy went tight and all *I* could manage was a squeak. My heart was going thump thump thump. I was about to meet Barney and be on television and it was so exciting – but oh-so-scary too. What if Barney didn't take any notice of me? What if I couldn't think of anything to say? I leaned forward and mumbled something of the sort into Mike's ear.

'You can't *help* noticing you, Tracy. And I've never *ever* known you at a loss for words,' he said.

We arrived at the studio and Mike ann-ounced to the doorman that we were Tracy Beaker and Party.

I loved that.

'I'm Tracy Beaker and you are my party!' I sang.

'You're Tracy Beaker and you are so *farty*,' sang Justine-Very-Vulgar-Littlewood.

We all had to get signed in, me and my party, and then we were led to a *dressing room*. I wanted it to have TRACY BEAKER, SUPERSTAR! on the door, but it just had a plain old number. Still, it was a very swish room, with a big mirror and two stylish sofas.

'Of course, this is pretty bog-standard compared with my *mum's* dressing rooms,' I said. 'She has white velvet sofas. They give her a new spotless one each week. And there's a chandelier and a white rug so soft she sinks in it up to her ankles.'

No one seemed to be listening to me, not even Peter. He was sucking his thumb, his chin on his chest.

'For goodness sake, Pete, you'll fuse all the cameras if you go into the studios with a face like that,' I said. I gave him a little prod. I wanted him to prod me back. He didn't. He just bent over further, his knees buckling.

'Come here, little pal,' said Mike, putting his arm round him. 'Don't worry about the hankie, I'm sure Jenny will find it for you. Or we'll get you another special hankie.'

'There isn't another one. Not one that belonged to my nan,' Peter mumbled around his thumb. 'It's all I've got left of her.'

Mike leaned over Peter's head, looking at me.

'Do you hear what he's saying, Tracy?' he said.

I didn't *want* to hear. My heart was still going

thump thump thump. Then there was a knock on my dressing room door and there was *Barney*!

'It's really *you*, Barney!' I gasped.

'No, actually I'm a cardboard cut-out,' he said, laughing. 'Hi, you must be Tracy.'

He picked me out! He knew me as soon as our eyes met!

'How did you know I'm Tracy?' I asked, thrilled.

'Oh, you're just how I imagined. And maybe your heart locket gave me a little bit of a clue. Oh dear though, Tracy, it looks a very special gold locket. I'm not sure we can let you swap it if it's really valuable.'

'No, it's fine, Barney. It's not solid gold,' I said hastily. 'It isn't really worth much, is it, Peter?'

Peter shook his head, his thumb still stoppering his mouth.

'And we're desperate to get that karaoke kit, aren't we, Peter?' I said.

Peter nodded this time, still mute.

'Well, we'll do our best to get it for you, kids,' said Barney. 'I think we're ready for you in the studio now. Come and meet Melvyn and Basil.'

We trooped along behind him. I hopped and skipped until I was beside him, staring up at him smiling and smiling and smiling.

'Are you excited about being on television, Tracy?' said Barney.

'You bet I am,' I said. I tried fluttering my eyelashes at him.

'Have you got something in your eyes, sweetheart?' said Barney. 'Try blinking hard.'

It was blinking hard trying to concentrate. I couldn't take my eyes off Barney and his soft hair and his big brown eyes and the little fuzzy down on his upper lip. My heart ached where the arrow had struck.

We trooped into the studio and stepped over snaky cables to the brightly coloured set. There were guys dressed up as lions and tigers and bears, a big Frosty the Snowman, children milling around, and a huge tank full of lime green gunge.

'A swimming pool!' Maxy yelled, hurtling towards it.

Mike managed to rugby-tackle him just as he was about to dive straight in.

'He's a game little chap,' said Barney, chuckling. 'But what's up with you, little guy?' He bent down to talk to Peter. 'Why are you all droopy-poopy? Don't you want to be on television?'

'*Tracy* wants to be on television,' Peter mumbled.

'And do you do what Tracy says, eh?' said Barney. 'Is she the boss?'

'She's not *my* boss,' said Justine-Can't-Bear-To-Be-Ignored-Littlewood.

'Tracy *is* a bit bossy,' said Peter. 'But I don't mind. She's my sweetheart.'

'Aah!' said Barney.

'I'm his sweetheart but he's not *mine*,' I whispered into Barney's ear.

Barney nodded though he didn't look as if he absolutely understood. But there was no time to elaborate as we were being prodded into position for the start of the show. I had to sit on a special chair beside Barney and Basil Brush popped up beside him.

'Oooh! It's a little doggy!' yelled Maxy.

'I am not a *dog*, little boy,' said Basil Brush, giving him a poke with his pointy snout. 'Why did the dog kennel leak, humm? It needed a new *woof*! Boom Boom!'

'Silly doggy,' said Maxy, unimpressed.

'Quit being a pain, Maxy,' said Justine-Interfering-Littlewood.

She stood right behind my chair, and when I peered round at her she was pouting at the camera in sick-making fashion. Louise was simpering too and Adele was striking a pose, hand on her hip.

Peter was standing a little apart. He reached for the bottom of his sweater and

held it awkwardly up to his nose, rubbing against it. He was so hopelessly lost without his nan's hankie. It was all he had left of her. Apart from the heart locket . . .

My own heart went thump thump thump.

'We're on air in ten seconds,' said Barney. 'Good luck, kids.'

My heart was thumping so hard I thought it would burst right out my sweater. The *Swap Shop* music started and Barney and Basil chatted away, welcoming everyone to the show.

'We're particularly delighted to welcome Tracy here, with all her friends—'

'And enemies,' muttered Justine-Can't-Shut-Up-Littlewood.

'—who live in a Children's Home and very much want a karaoke machine to have fun with,' said Barney. 'So what have you got to swap, Tracy?'

'I've got this very special unique gold locket,' I said, holding it up.

'And who gave it to you?' said Barney.

'My friend Peter gave it to me on Valentine's Day,' I said.

Justine and Louise made yuck noises behind my back. Peter put his hand up, trying valiantly to smile.

'So you two are little lovebirds, eh?' said Barney.

'What do you call two birds in love?' asked Basil Brush. 'Soppy! Boom boom!'

'I think they're very sweet,' said Barney. 'So who gave *you* this lovely locket, Peter?'

'It was my nan's,' Peter whispered. Two tears spilled down his cheeks.

'Oh, Peter, *don't* cry,' I said.

'I'm not crying, Tracy. I – I've just got hayfever,' Peter snuffled.

I looked at him. My heart gave such a thump I had to clutch my chest. What was the matter with me? Why were there tears in my own eyes? I was Tracy Beaker, tough as old boots. Why was I worrying so? The silly old locket wasn't worth anything.

I couldn't kid myself any more. The locket was worth the whole world to Peter – and he'd given it to me.

'I can't *do* this!' I wailed. 'I'm sorry, Barney. Please don't get mad at me. I know I'm wrecking your programme and I so want a karaoke machine but I *can't* swap the heart. It's all Peter's got left of his nan now. It's maybe not actually *real* gold but that doesn't matter, it's worth much more because it was so special to him and yet he gave it to me. So now I'm going to give it back to him. Here you are, Pete.' I took it off and handed it to him.

'Oh, Tracy! We wanted the karaoke machine!' said Justine-No-Heart-At-All-Littlewood.

'Well, maybe we can see if you can *win* a karaoke machine,' said Barney. 'We've got our three teams set up to brave the dreaded Gungulator. How about you guys challenging the winners? Just two of you. Let's see – Tracy and Justine!'

'But we can't be in a team *together*! We're deadly enemies,' I protested.

'There's no way I'm ever being part of a team with *Tracy*,' said Justine. 'I'll be in a team with Louise.'

'No, no, Peter and me will be a team!' I insisted.

'Count *me* out of any team. I'm not going in that green gunge!' said Adele in horror.

'I'll go, I'll go, I *love* green gunge,' Maxy shouted.

'Hey, hey, shh you lot. Do you want to give it a go or not?' said Barney. He grinned at me. He grinned at Justine. 'Go on, girls. Swallow your differences.'

I didn't want to let Barney down. I looked at Justine. She looked at me. We both swallowed. Then we nodded.

So we sat and watched the rest of the show. Peter nestled right up to me, the heart locket round his neck.

'You can have it back though, Tracy. It *is* yours,' he whispered.

'We'll share it, Pete, OK. Now be quiet, I need to watch this game to see how it works.'

One kid got in a bed on a trolley. The other kid shoved the bed. They scored points the further it went. But if the shove was too hard then the bed went right off the scale and the kid tipped straight into the green slime.

We watched, we waited, we wondered . . . The Zebras team were defeated first. Then the Bees. So we had to beat the Tigers – with a final score of 100.

'We'll beat that easy-peasy,' I said to Justine.

'Of course we will,' she said.

'Good luck, Tracy!' said Peter.

'Good luck, Justine!' said Louise.

'Good luck both of you,' said Barney. 'Right, Tracy, you get on the bed first.' I got on the bed and Justine stood behind me.

'Watch what you're doing now, Justine. Don't be too feeble. Give a really firm push – but not *too* hard!'

'Oh, quit bossing me, Tracy Beaker,' Justine snapped and gave my bed a shove.

I shot forward. I passed 50, then 100, 150 . . . I was slowing now, and I so needed to slow! I pulled hard on the end of the bed, trying to brake, but it was no use. I was edging further and further forward, past 200, past 250, past 500, oh no, past 750 and then . . .

SPLASH!

I screamed and swallowed a bucketful of icy-cold lime-green slime. I struggled to my feet, shaking my head, while the whole studio collapsed with laughter around me. *Right!* I'd show that Justine-Totally-Did-It-On-Purpose-Littlewood. In thirty seconds she'd be drenched in slime herself and see how *she* liked it.

I heaved myself out of the pool, snorting slime. Justine was practically wetting herself.

'Oh, help, it's a green slime sludge monster! No, wait a minute, it's Tracy Beaker!'

'You wait!' I said, as she clambered onto the bed and I took charge of the controls.

'Remember, Tracy, you want that karaoke set,' Barney called quickly. 'If Justine goes in the slime you'll lose your chance of winning one!'

My heart went . . . you've got it, thump thump thump! I sooo wanted to dump Justine in the green gunge the way she'd dumped me. But if I did then we'd lose our karaoke set and I sooo wanted that too. Not just for me. Peter and I could sing our duets . . .

I looked at Peter.

'Go for it, Tracy!' he yelled.

'Yeah, crack it, girl!' Adele shouted.

'Yes yes yes!' Maxy burbled.

'You can do it, Tracy,' said Mike.

'Do it for everyone, Tracy,' said Barney, giving me the thumbs-up sign.

I took a deep breath and gave Justine a sharp edgy shove that set her rolling. She went past 50, 100, 150, 200 . . . She was yelling like crazy now, ducking her head – but then she slowed to a dramatic halt, spot on the 250 sign. We'd beaten the others! Yay, we'd won!!!

'Well done, Tracy! You've won your karaoke machine for you and all your mates. I knew you could do it!' Barney shouted happily.

'I knew I could too!' I said. My heart went thumpety-thumpety-thump and I gave him a great big hug. 'So we've really won it, no matter what? No going back on it?'

'Yes, really,' said Barney.

'Great!' I said – and before Justine-Ever-Deadly-Enemy-Littlewood could get out of the bed I gave it one more shove. She shot straight into the green gunge. That wiped the grin off her face!

THE
MUM-MINDER

To the Dimwits who aren't dim at all,
but are very witty

☆ MONDAY ☆

It's half-term. No more stupid, boring, silly old school for a whole week! Oh-oh. Maybe that's not tactful seeing as this is a school project. We've all got to keep a holiday diary. I've got to hand this in next Monday. I can't rub it out because it's written with my mum's biro and it would just make great blue smears all over the page. My baby sister Sara chewed my own pen up yesterday. My special red felt-tip pen which also doubles as a lipstick if I'm dressing up. Sara's not got all her teeth yet but she can't half chew. She looked like Dracula with all this red ink dripping down her chin.

I felt really cross with her but that's babies for you. I get more than a bit fed up with babies sometimes. I am surrounded by them right this minute. Three-year-old Gemma keeps pulling at my arm, wanting me to draw for her. Two-year-old Vincent is drawing himself, making horrible scribbles on the back of a paper bag. Baby Clive is having a yell because Mum's put him down for a nap and he doesn't feel like it. And Sara's sitting on my foot, bouncing up and down, wanting a ride.

They're not all my brothers and sisters. No fear. My sister Sara's quite enough to be going on with.

No, my mum's a childminder. She doesn't have to mind me. I'm Sadie and I'm nearly nine. I can mind myself, easy-peasy. I can look after Sara too. I sometimes get up in the night and give her a bottle. And I play with her and I take her out for a walk in her push chair. I do a lot of things for my mum and all. I make her a cup of tea when she's tired and I've got this knack of massaging her feet which she loves.

'I don't know what I'd do without you, Sadie,' she says.

We don't see much of my dad nowadays, but it doesn't matter.

'Us girls will stick together, eh?' says Mum, and sometimes I climb up on her lap as well as Sara and we all have a big hug together.

I quite like my mum being a childminder because she's always there when I get home from school. The only trouble is in the holidays. Babies don't have holidays. They don't have half-terms either. Mum gets lumbered with them all the time.

If it was just Mum and me then this half-term would be great. We could go down to the shops and look round at all the clothes and the toys and choose what we'd buy if we had all the money in the world. Or we could go to the Leisure Centre and have a swim in the pool. They've got a big wave machine and all my friends say it's smashing. Or we could play that I'm a lady too and we could go and have a pot of tea and a Danish pastry each and have a good gossip in a proper restaurant. But you can't go shopping or swimming or eating when you've got four babies. My sister Sara would be bad enough. But if we've got Gemma and Vincent and little Clive as well then it's impossible.

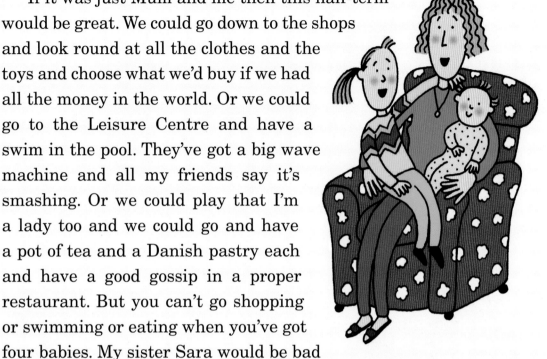

Nan usually helps. She acts as Mum's assistant. She's got another job working in a pub at nights but she doesn't mind giving Mum a hand too. You need lots and lots of hands with all those babies. But Nan phoned up this morning and said she couldn't make it. Grandad's off work with the flu. My grandad's like a great big baby himself. Nan's going to be busy looking after him for a few days.

'Never mind, Mum. *I'll* be your assistant,' I said. 'Good job I'm off school, eh?'

So I've done my best. It hasn't been easy. Especially when we went out for a walk and called in at the corner shop. Mum uses a double buggy and I carried Sara but it was still a job carting them around.

And then Sara started shrieking in the shop because she wanted Smarties, and Gemma picked a packet of jelly off the shelf and wouldn't let go, and Vincent went rushing round the corner and barged straight into a

pile of toilet rolls and knocked them all over the place, and Clive yelled his head off all the time.

He's been yelling all day. It doesn't half get on your nerves. It's given Mum a headache. She looks ever so white and tired. Hang on. I know what I'll do.

Later

Well, I've made Mum a cup of tea. She's had a couple of aspirins too, though they don't look as if they're helping much. I've given Clive another bottle and he's got off to sleep. I've sat on the sofa with the others and read them this story about Dominic the Vole. Dominic the Vole is fat and funny and he's always getting into trouble. (Very like my little sister Sara.) Gemma liked the story and wanted me to read it again, but Vincent got fidgety and Sara kept wanting to hold the book herself but when I let her she bit right into it. Dominic the Vole has got teethmarks across his bottom now.

'You're being the childminder today, Sadie,' Mum said. 'I'd better give you half my wages.'

'Are you feeling better now, Mum?'

'Yes,' said Mum, but she didn't sound sure. She sneezed suddenly.

'You sound as if you're getting a cold, Mum,' I said.

'No I'm not,' said Mum, and then she sneezed again. She blew her nose. 'Just a little sniffle, that's all. I'm OK. I'll take over the kids now, Sadie. You can go out and play.'

Later still

I had a good game with my friend Rachel up the road, but I kept looking in on Mum. She looked whiter than ever and she was shivering. The babies were all being very boisterous. I knew Mum was longing to get shot of them all. Well, she's got to put up with Sara all the time, but that can't be helped.

Clive's mum usually comes first because her chocolate shop closes at half-past five. But she's going to a babywear party tonight so she asked Mum to have him for the whole evening. And then Vincent's mum rang up and said the trains were up the spout and she'd be late getting back from the office to pick him up. And then, to crown it all, Gemma's mum phoned to say she'd arrested someone – she's a policewoman, you see – and she'd probably be an hour or so later than planned.

'That's OK,' Mum said to Clive's mum and Vincent's mum and Gemma's mum.

'But you don't feel well, Mum,' I said.

'Us girls have got to stick together,' said Mum.

So she looked after all the babies. I put Sara to bed and then, by the time we'd got rid of Vincent and Gemma and at long last Clive, Mum said she felt so shattered she wanted to go to bed too.

She was so tired I had to help her undress and then I tucked her up under the covers and gave her a kiss.

'You're being a mum-minder now,' said Mum.

☆ TUESDAY ☆

We didn't get off to a good start today. Sara was awake half the night and Mum had to keep getting up to her. So she was so tired she slept right through her alarm and we didn't wake up until Vincent's mum rang the doorbell.

'Oh no,' said Mum.

Something seemed to have happened to her voice overnight. She sounded more like my dad than my mum.

She stumbled downstairs in her nightie, croaking to me to put the kettle on. Sara started yelling for attention so I put my head round her door.

'Ook,' she said proudly.

She was standing up in her cot, hanging on to the rail, bouncing her fat little feet. She'd managed to unpop her pyjamas *and* her nappy. She suddenly stood still and started weeing, a look of wonder on her face.

'Sara!' I shouted, and snatched her out of the cot but I was several seconds too late. It looked like the whole of Sara's bedding was going to have to go in the washing machine.

'You're a bad girl. Poor Mum's feeling rotten and you're just making things worse for her,' I said severely. 'Yup,' said Sara, and giggled.

I bundled her under one arm and went downstairs to see to the kettle. Vincent's mum was in the kitchen, stalking about in her high heels, looking a bit tetchy because we were in such a muddle. She was holding Vincent warily, not wanting him to dribble down her smart suit. Vincent is getting a back tooth and has turned into a human waterfall.

'Sorry I overslept,' Mum mumbled. 'Here, I'll take Vincent. You get off to work now, you don't want to be late.'

'Yes, well, I have got this very important meeting this morning,' said Vincent's mum, but she looked at my mum a bit worriedly. 'Are you all right? You don't look very well,' she said, absent-mindedly slotting Vincent into the highchair in the kitchen.

Sara started shrieking indignantly in my arms. It's her highchair and she doesn't care to share it. Vincent started shouting too because his mum wasn't watching what she was doing and was bending one of his legs backwards.

'I'm fine,' said Mum, unhooking Vincent's leg and taking the struggling Sara from me.

'You don't look fine,' said Vincent's mum.

'I've just got a little sniffle, that's all,' said Mum.

Vincent's mum didn't look convinced, but she had her important meeting so she whisked off sharpish.

Mum let Sara slide off her lap and rested her head in her arms.

'I think you'd better go back to bed, Mum,' I said.

'No, I'm OK, love, really,' said Mum. 'Well, I will be when I've had a nice cup of tea.'

Gemma and her mum turned up while we were still having breakfast. Gemma's mum let me try on her police hat while she had a cup of tea too. I frisked Gemma and cautioned Vincent and made some handcuffs out of tinfoil and captured Sara but she simply chewed her way free.

Mum had two cups of tea and said she felt much better. She didn't look better at all. She was white with black rings round her eyes, just like Sara's toy panda.

She was still sneezing.

'Sorry about my cold,' Mum sniffed. 'I'll try not to give it to the kids.'

'You sound as if you've got a bit more than a cold,' said Gemma's mum. 'I feel a bit mean leaving you to cope, especially as your mum can't come. But I've got to go to court this morning, so I've really got to leave Gemma with you.'

'That's all right. We'll manage, don't worry,' said Mum, and she looked at me.

I sighed. It looked like I was going to be reading *Dominic the Vole* until I was blue in the face.

Gemma's mum pushed off and Mum crawled away to get washed and dressed. She tried putting on a bit of make-up so that she didn't look so bad, but it just looked weird: white face, black eyes and bright red lipstick. Mum's nose was getting red to match because she was having to wipe it so often.

'It's just a little cold. I won't breathe on the baby,' Mum told Clive's mum.

'I think my Clive's got a bit of a cold himself,' said Clive's mum. 'He's in a bit of a bad mood today. Got the grizzles and won't stop.'

'Oh,' said Mum weakly, and rubbed her forehead.

'Have you got a headache?' said Clive's mum.

'Just a bit,' said Mum.

'Are you sure you haven't got flu?' said Clive's mum. 'There's a lot of it about.'

'No, no,' said Mum. 'Of course I haven't.'

Clive's mum went off to her chocolate shop and we were left with all the babies.

'Don't worry, I'll give you a hand, Mum,' I said, but then my friend Rachel from up the road came round to see if I wanted to go over to her house to watch videos.

'I can't really. I've got to help my mum because she's not feeling well,' I said.

'I'm feeling fine,' Mum said determinedly. 'You go round to Rachel's and have a bit of fun, Sadie.'

So I did. Rachel and I watched a Walt Disney video and then her dad went out to do the shopping and we watched this really scary monster video instead, fast forwarding through the worst bits. Then we took turns being the Monster Blob and obliterating each other, and I was having such good fun I forgot all about Mum and the Monster Blobby Babies.

I was very late getting back. And oh dear. Clive was in his carrycot, bellowing fit to bust. Gemma had the television turned up too loud and was fiddling with the knobs to make it even louder. Vincent was crayoning all over the wall with Mum's red lipstick. Sara had chewed an entire corner off the *Dominic the Vole* book so that his little snout and one whole paw were missing. And Mum was sitting in the middle of the floor with great big tears running down her cheeks.

'I don't think I am fine after all,' she sobbed. 'And I phoned Nan to see if she can take over tomorrow but Grandad's really bad and she's starting to sneeze all over the place herself.'

I felt ever so ever so ever so mean. I hadn't helped Mum one little bit.

Gemma's mum finished at court early and came round to see how Mum was.

She took one look and shook her head.

'You've definitely got flu. Go on up to bed this instant. I'll look after the kids until the other mums get here. Sadie will help me, won't you, pal?'

'Yes, of course.'

'Well, all right then,' Mum groaned. 'But I'll be better tomorrow, I promise.'

'That's nonsense,' said Gemma's mum. 'You'll have to take to your bed and stay there.'

'But what about the babies?' said Mum, sniffling.

'We'll sort something out, won't we, Sadie?' said Gemma's mum.

'You bet,' I said. 'Us girls have got to stick together.'

☆ WEDNESDAY ☆

You'll never guess what! I've been a *real* policewoman today. Gemma's mum took me to work with her. And her Gemma. And our Sara. And Vincent and little Clive. All of us.

My mum has got flu. Gemma's mum drove her to the doctor's last night. Mum's got to stay in bed today and tomorrow and the next day. So has Nan. She's got it too.

'I can't have flu. I'm never ill,' Mum moaned. 'I can't let you all down. I've got to look after the kids.'

'Well, you *are* ill, whether we like it or not,' said Gemma's mum. 'And you've never let us down before. You've always looked after our kids. So we've got to stick together, like Sadie said.'

'That's right. And it's OK. *I'll* look after the babies,' I said. I was feeling bad about leaving Mum to cope on her own and I was desperate to make up for it.

'It's sweet of you to offer, Sadie, but you're only a kid yourself, love,' said Gemma's mum.

I got a bit annoyed at that. I'm not a kid, I'm nearly nine for goodness sake, and Mum says I'm old for my age. I look after Sara enough times. If you can cope with our Sara then other babies are a doddle. Gemma's quite a sensible little kid at times, and Vincent's OK if you keep an eye on him – well, two eyes plus one in the back of your head – and baby Clive doesn't yell *all* the time.

But Gemma's mum and Vincent's mum and Clive's mum and even *my* mum wouldn't listen to me. They said I couldn't cope.

'We're the ones who are going to have to cope,' said Gemma's mum. 'But how?' said Vincent's mum. 'I can't leave Vincent with a neighbour because they go out to work too.'

'My mother-in-law always said she'd look after any babies if I had to go back to work, but the first time she looked after Clive he cried all the time and she said Never Again,' said Clive's mum. 'She just couldn't manage.'

'We're going to have to manage,' said Gemma's mum. 'It's only for this week. Can't anyone take three days off work? I would, but I've used up all my leave.'

Vincent's mum and Clive's mum couldn't take time off either.

'Then just this once we'll have to take the kids to work with us,' said Gemma's mum.

'How on earth could I have the babies in my office?' said Vincent's mum.

'You can't have kids cooped up behind the chocolate counter all day,' said Clive's mum.

'I'll look after them as usual,' my mum croaked. 'I can go to bed when they have their naps and—'

'Nonsense,' said Gemma's mum. 'Now listen. Tomorrow *I'll* have the kids. They can come to the police station with me. Then Thursday they can go uptown to your office and Friday go to the shop. I know it's going to be difficult but we'll just have to give it a whirl.'

I still feel like I'm whirling. And it's great great great!

I got up ever so early and gave Sara a baby bottle to keep her quiet while I got washed and dressed, and then I made Mum a cup of tea and some toast for her breakfast. Then I heated up some tomato soup at the same time and poured it in to a vacuum flask.

'That's your lunch, Mum,' I explained, when I'd woken her and propped a couple of pillows behind her. 'And look, I've brought some apples and biscuits up, and the kettle and the coffee and Sara's Ribena because I think you need the vitamin C more than she does.'

'You're a real pal, Sadie,' Mum mumbled. 'So where are you going today then? Round to Rachel's?'

'You must be joking! I'll have to go to the police station with Gemma's mum. She'll never cope with the babies on her own.'

You can say that again.

She looked a bit fussed when she came to pick us up.

'Me and my big mouth,' she said. 'I haven't a clue what my boss is going to say. I don't *think* there's anything in Police Orders about not bringing your children and all their little friends to work with you, but I kind of get the feeling it's going to be frowned on.'

Gemma's mum's Police Inspector boss did frown when he saw all of us. His eyebrows practically knitted together.

'What on earth are you playing at, WPC Parsons?' he said.

'Oh, Sir,' said Gemma's mum, and she started gabbling this long, involved, apologetic explanation, while Gemma scuffed her shoes and Vincent picked his nose and Sara struggled in my arms and Clive cried in his carrycot.

'This is ridiculous,' said the Inspector. 'You're a policewoman, not Mary Blooming Poppins. I can't have my police station turned into a nursery, not even for one day. You must take them all home with you right this minute.'

Sara had stopped struggling. She was staring up at the Inspector. Then she gave him a big sunny smile.

'Dad-Dad!' she announced delightedly.

The Inspector looked shocked.

'I'm not your Dad-Dad,' he said.

'*Dad-Dad!*' Sara insisted, and held out her chubby arms to him.

It's not her fault. We don't often see our dad. Sara's only little and she makes mistakes.

The Inspector was big and he looked as if he'd never made a mistake in his life – but he made one right that minute. His arms reached out of their own accord. Sara snuggled up to him happily.

'Dad-Dad,' she announced smugly, patting his cheek.

He still tried to frown, but he couldn't stop his mouth going all smiley.

'Is this your little girl, WPC Parsons?' he asked.

'No, Sir. This one's mine. Gemma. Say hello to the Inspector, Gemma,' said Gemma's mum.

Gemma wasn't going to let Sara get all the attention. She smiled determinedly at the Inspector, tossing her curls.

'Hello, Mr Inspector Man. I've come to work with Mummy.'

'Well. Just for today,' said the Inspector, picking her up too.

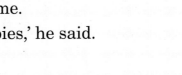

Gemma's mum winked at me. It looked like it was going to be OK after all.

'How would you like a ride in my police car, eh?' said the Inspector.

'Me too, me too, me too!' said Vincent, tugging at the Inspector's trouser leg.

Clive let out a long, loud wail from his carrycot.

'He's practising being a police siren,' I said.

The Inspector looked at me.

'You're not one of the babies,' he said.

'I should think not,' I said indignantly. 'I'm here to keep them all in order.'

'I'm glad to hear it. It looks as if it's going to be some undertaking,' said the Inspector. 'We'd better give you a bit of authority.'

He found me a policewoman's hat and a special tie and a big badge. 'There we go. Now you're head of my Child Protection Team. What's your name?'

'Sadie. Sir,' I added, and I gave him a little salute.

'I'm glad you've reported for duty, WPC Sadie,' he said. 'Right, I'll give you your orders. Quieten the baby. Wipe the little boy's nose – my trousers are getting rather damp. And take these two little treasures from me so I can give you a proper salute back.'

Gemma jumped down happily enough but Sara screamed when I tried to take her.

'Dad-Dad!' she insisted furiously and that poor nice-after-all Inspector had to carry her around all day long.

We had a wonderful time. The Inspector really did take us out in a big police car. He wouldn't go very fast but he did put the siren on just for a second. That was another mistake. Vincent made very loud police-siren noises all day after that, and Clive did his best to accompany him.

We had Coke and crisps back in the police canteen and then, when Gemma's mum had to do some work, the Inspector took us to see a great big

police dog. Gemma didn't like him
and Vincent was a bit worried,
but Sara laughed and patted
him.

'Yes, nice doggy,' said the
Inspector.

'Nice Dad-Dad,' said Sara.

She's dead artful, my little baby sister. Like I said, she insisted
on staying with the Inspector, even when he had to parade some
policemen and inspect some prisoners in the cells. Sara smiled all
the time and the policemen and even the prisoners smiled back.

Gemma and Vincent were both getting a bit restless
– and baby Clive was very restless indeed. I was
tempted to leave him in one of the prisoners' cells,
but one of the canteen ladies plucked him up in
her arms and started cooing at him. She gave him
a little lick of her special syrup pudding and it
sweetened him up considerably.

I left Clive with the canteen
lady and played prisoners with
Gemma and Vincent, and a friendly
police man showed me how to take their
fingerprints with wonderful gungy black ink.
Vincent particularly enjoyed the procedure.
He didn't just put his fingerprints on the pad.
He put them on his knees and his nose and
the desk and even up the wall.

The friendly policeman had to carry him

off to be scrubbed. I paraded Gemma up and down the corridors and into the control-room and another friendly policeman showed us how to work his computer so that lots of squiggly green information flashed up on the screen. Gemma thought it was better than television and sat on his lap and had a go at pressing all the buttons herself.

I left Gemma with that friendly policeman and went to see what my fellow policewoman was up to. Gemma's mum was in the front office seeing to members of the public. She let me stand up on a box and see to them too. We took particulars of a stolen purse and Gemma's mum showed me how to fill in a crime sheet. She said I did it very neatly. I think it's all the practice writing in this diary. I've been writing and writing and writing today since we got back home.

Mum's in bed. Sara's in bed too. She was still saying Dad-Dad as she drifted off to sleep. That Inspector says he's not her Dad-Dad but perhaps he could be a sort of uncle and come and visit her some time.

He's not a bit frowny and fierce when you get to know him. I think I'll maybe go and work full-time for him when I'm grown up.

☆ THURSDAY ☆

Us girls didn't really stick together today. But it didn't matter. We still had a lot of fun. And Mum had another day in bed. She said if only she didn't feel ill it would be Absolute Bliss.

Vincent's mum looked as if she was undergoing Abject Torture. She came to collect us all with Vincent's dad. He was tall and twinkly and as soon as she spotted him Sara tried her Dad-Dad trick. It didn't work this time.

'*My* dad,' said Vincent fiercely, and when Sara tried to crawl up Vincent's dad's smartly suited trouser leg, Vincent gave her a shove so that she sat down with a thump. I don't think it hurt because her bottom's well padded with nappy, but she yelled a lot.

Vincent's dad just tutted, but Vincent's mum was horrified and told Vincent that he was a very naughty, unkind little boy and he mustn't push little girls over.

Vincent screwed up his face and looked as if he'd like to push his big mummy over. We all went to the railway station to catch the train to London. Vincent's mum and Vincent's dad and Vincent and Gemma and Clive and Sara and me. We had the double buggy and we'd started off with Vincent and Clive strapped in, Gemma holding Vincent's mum's hand, and me carrying Sara. Vincent's dad didn't seem too keen to hold or carry anyone so he just pushed the buggy.

Sara was very annoyed about this.

It's our buggy and she decided she ought to be sitting in it. Vincent started struggling to get out of the buggy once we got on the platform, so Vincent's mum plucked him out and popped Sara in his place. This wasn't as sensible as it seemed. Vincent shot off like a rocket up the platform to look for trains. Vincent's dad fielded him niftily but then handed him over firmly to Vincent's mum. She tried taking Clive out of the buggy this time and strapped Vincent back in beside Sara. Vincent yelled furiously and kicked out, trying to escape. He kicked Sara by accident and she screamed. Baby Clive cried too, just to be companionable.

Vincent's dad moved a few paces away and got out his newspaper. 'Aren't the babies being naughty,' said Gemma, squeezing Vincent's mum's hand.

Vincent's mum looked as if she were about to cry too.

'I can't have them creating this sort of chaos in my office,' she said anxiously.

'Don't worry. They were ever so good at the police station yesterday,' I said, trying to reassure her.

'Well, I don't know what on earth you were all up to, but my Vincent came home absolutely filthy. He left the most terrible fingermarks all over my cream upholstery. Vincent! Vincent, will you *stop* that silly screaming. And you, Sara. Is she always like this, Sadie? And why is the baby screeching his head off?' She held Clive as if he was a ticking bomb.

'Can't you stop him making such a noise?' Vincent's dad muttered from behind his newspaper.

'Honestly, what do you expect me to do?' said Vincent's mum crossly. 'Babies don't have volume control, you know.'

'He likes it if you jiggle him about a bit,' I said helpfully.

Vincent's mum jiggled Clive.

Perhaps she jiggled him a jot too much. He was sick all down his front. He was sick down quite a lot of Vincent's mum's front too.

'Oh no,' said Vincent's mum, dabbing at the

damp bits with a tissue. 'Pooh, he smells now,' said Gemma. Clive revved up his crying, obviously insulted. Vincent and Sara were feeling ignored and so they yelled louder. Then the train rushed into the station and Gemma got startled and she started crying too.

All the other people on the platform scrambled to get into other carriages. Nobody seemed to want to sit with us. Vincent's dad looked as if he might get into another carriage too, but he manoeuvred the buggy on to the train while Vincent's mum and I hauled in all the babies. They all shut up when the train started, except Gemma. She decided she was very seriously scared of trains. She had to sit on Vincent's mum's lap. Vincent's mum's skirt got very seriously creased.

'I must be mad,' she muttered distractedly. 'Why did I ever say I'd do this?'

'Because us girls have got to stick together,' I said brightly.

'That's all very well. But how can I be taken seriously as a professional working woman when I've got five frightful kids fighting in my office?' Vincent's mum wailed.

'*Four* kids,' I said indignantly. 'I'm here to help you.'

'Quite right, Sadie,' said Vincent's dad, twinkling at me over the top of his newspaper.

'You can shut up for a start,' said Vincent's mum.

'Now now. Temper temper. I don't know why you're getting in such a state. You've only got to look after the children for one measly little day,' said Vincent's dad. 'I'm sure you can fit them into a corner of your office, give them some paper to crayon on, let them make necklaces out of paperclips— When you think about it, the average office is a wonderful playland for kids. You've just got to use your initiative.'

Vincent's mum squared her shoulders inside her smart suit.

'Well, I'm going to use my initiative right now,' she said, as the train drew into the station. 'If you think it's such a doddle then *you* look after the children.'

She opened the carriage door and was off down the platform, her high heels twinkling. We all peered after her, our mouths open. Vincent's dad's jaw was positively sagging.

'Mummy gone,' Vincent announced, in case we hadn't quite grasped the situation.

'Oh dear,' said Gemma. 'I liked that lady.'

'I don't like her at all,' said Vincent's dad. 'I can't believe this. How can she do this to me?'

'Maybe she'll be back in a minute,' I said helpfully. 'Maybe she's just giving you a little fright.'

She was succeeding too. Vincent's dad had gone pale and lost all his twinkle.

'What am I going to do?' he murmured wretchedly after I'd unloaded everyone and the buggy on to the platform and we'd stood around waiting for five or ten minutes. It was getting obvious that Vincent's mum really had scarpered.

'We'll have to go to your office,' I said. 'We'll fit into a corner, like you said. And we can crayon and I can make them all the paperclip necklaces and it'll be like a playland.'

'Playland! I want to go to playland!' said Gemma.

'Playland, playland,' said Vincent.

'Play!' said Sara.

'Pa-pa-pa,' said Clive.

'I wish I'd kept my big mouth shut,' said Vincent's dad.

He wouldn't attempt to take us to his office by tube. He bundled us into a taxi.

'Are you a new kind of nanny, Gov?' said the taxi driver.

'Certainly not,' said Vincent's dad, struggling to keep control of his son while our Sara tore his newspaper into shreds and baby Clive yelled because he didn't know where he was going.

Gemma and I sat up straight and looked out of the windows, as good as gold.

'Is Playland nice, Sadie?' Gemma asked.

'I hope so,' I said.

Vincent's dad worked in a great glass building. His office was right at the top so we had to go up in a big lift. It went fast and we all held our tummies and sucked in air through our teeth. Even Clive stopped squawking and hissed in astonishment, not sure whether he liked this new sensation or not.

Vincent's dad worked in a great big room with huge windows.

'They don't open easily, do they?' I said. I am very responsible about child safety. Vincent's dad didn't seem to appreciate this at all.

'If they did open then I think I'd throw myself out,' he said. 'Look at them!'

Gemma and Vincent and Sara and Clive had instantly made themselves at home. They'd taken Vincent's dad at his word. It really was Playland.

Gemma had recognized the computer on the desk and was stabbing happily and haphazardly at the buttons.

Vincent had found a fat felt-tip pen and was decorating a pile of official papers with yellow scribble.

Sara had overturned a big pot plant and was making a mud pie on the carpet.

Clive was lying on his back exercising his lungs, as he was still too little to play properly.

Vincent's dad groaned and called feebly for his secretary.

'I am prepared to pay you a double wage today, Karen, so long as you take these dreadful children off my hands,' he said weakly.

Karen giggled. 'Ah yes. Your wife's just sent a fax to see if the children are all right.'

'The children are fine, as you can see. I'm the one who is suffering. I'd like a black coffee and two aspirin, please.'

I helped Karen round everyone up.

She took us to the typing pool. Gemma got disappointed because she thought she'd be able to paddle in this new pool, but she soon perked up when she saw all the word processors. She climbed on and off the typists' laps, playing with these lovely new machines.

All the typists made a great fuss of Vincent too. He ordered them about just like his dad. They sat him up on a desk with a pen and a memo pad and called him Sir.

They found a special job for Sara. The office paper-shredder was on the blink so they sat Sara down with all the unwanted paper and Sara tore and tore and tore it all into shreds. You could soon barely spot her under a great mound of scrumpled paper.

I palled up with the tealady and went all round the huge building with her, giving out all the cups of tea from her trolley. I could eat as many buns and biscuits as I wanted. I took Clive with me and whenever he got restless I just zapped him into a lift and took him for a quick trip up to the top and back.

When we'd finished the tea-round, the tealady took Clive over for a bit and I lay on top of the emptied tea trolley, kicked off with my feet and went whizzing along the corridor. It was better than the biggest skateboard. I nearly ran over Vincent's dad when he stepped out of his office but he managed to leap out of the way just in time.

He had a right cheek. Vincent's mum turned up at lunchtime, saying she'd got all her work done so she'd take us over for the afternoon. Vincent's dad acted as if he'd looked after us single-handed, and Vincent's mum said she was sorry and she thought he was splendid and when my mum was well enough to babysit she'd take him out for a slap-up meal to say thank you.

Vincent's mum took Vincent and Gemma and Clive and our Sara and me to a McDonald's for our lunch, which was great, and then she took us to a proper playground. Vincent's mum sat on a bench and did some of her paperwork while I pushed everyone on the swings and then we all sat in the sandpit and made sandcastles. Whenever anyone started crying, Vincent's mum bought ice-creams from a nearby van. We ended up having three or maybe it was four ice-creams, even Clive.

Clive wasn't the only one who was sick on the train going home.

☆ FRIDAY ☆

Mum's a bit better. She was worried when she heard about the argy-bargy between Vincent's mum and Vincent's dad.

'I think I'd better get back to looking after all the children today,' Mum said, and she got up for breakfast.

'Oh Mum, don't be silly. You still seem very fluey to me,' I said.

'I certainly *look* a bit fluey,' said Mum, running her fingers through her straggly hair and rubbing her poor red nose. 'But I still think it's time I took over. It sounds as if you're all running wild.'

'Grrr,' I said, baring my teeth and making my hands into claws.

'Grrr,' Sara copied, biting her breakfast banana very savagely.

'Anyway, Mum, you can't take over today. We'll miss out on all the fun,' I said tactlessly. 'I can't wait to go to Clive's mum's chocolate shop. Yum yum yum.'

'Yum yum,' said Sara, slobbering.

'Yes, that's what I'm worried about,' said Mum. 'Sara was sick yesterday. I don't want her eating lots of chocolate today and getting sick again.'

'It's OK, Mum. I'll look after her. I'm the mum-minder now and I'm supposed to be looking after you. So you go back to bed. You look all white and wobbly.'

'I do feel a bit shaky. All right then, Sadie.'

'That's a good mum,' I said. 'Back to bed. I'll come and tuck you up in a minute.'

We both giggled because everything was back to front and it sounded so funny, me telling Mum what to do. I don't want Mum to stay ill, but I wish I could always boss her around!

Clive's mum could do with being a bit bossier. She's little, not all that much bigger than me, and I bet I weigh more. I know if I worked in a chocolate shop I'd grow very big indeed. It's such a wonderful shop. Just the rich, creamy, chocolaty smell makes your mouth start watering. Clive's mum showed us all round the big glass cabinets piled high with hazelnut truffles and white whirly creams, strawberry marzipans and violet fondants, sugar mice and chocolate teddies.

'Can I have a chocolate teddy?' Gemma asked, reaching out. 'Chocolate ted!' Vincent demanded, grabbing.

'Choc choc!' said Sara, scrabbling.

'No, wait a minute! You mustn't touch, dears. Gemma, put it down, darling. Vincent, no! And look at Sara, she's dribbling all over the display,' said Clive's mum, dashing from one to the other.

Clive decided he wanted his mum's attention for himself.

'Oh dear. I don't know why he's crying, he's only just had his bottle,' said Clive's mum. 'Look, Gemma dear, I don't really think your mummy would like you to have *another* chocolate teddy. Vincent, don't touch those chocolate boxes! Oh dear, Sara. No, poppet, take it out of your mouth.'

I sussed out a stock-room at the back, with big empty cardboard boxes. I grabbed Sara and Gemma and lifted them into one box. It was more of a struggle with Vincent, but I eventually seized hold of him under the armpits and hauled him into the back room and caged him in another cardboard box.

'You're all wild animals in the zoo,' I said quickly. 'And it's feeding time. I'm the keeper and I've just fed you, right? You've got to growl back at me, grrrr, grrrr.'

'Grrr,' said Sara, who was used to this game.

Luckily, Gemma and Vincent thought it was fun too. They gnawed their stolen chocolate and growled contentedly. Clive did his best to play, roaring magnificently. He was a little too young for a cardboard cage and he was only allowed the merest lick of chocolate,

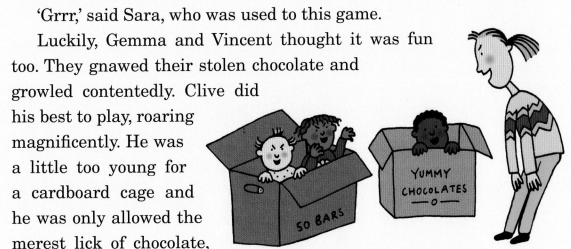

so I carried him round and round the shop to quieten him down.

'You're such a good girl, Sadie. You've got them all sorted out in no time,' said Clive's mum gratefully. 'Here, you'd better help yourself to a chocolate too.'

I rather hoped she'd offer me one. I wanted to show how grown up I am so I tried a liqueur chocolate. I was a bit disappointed in the taste. I hoped I'd get drunk. I started swaying about the shop experimentally and baby Clive chuckled, enjoying getting jiggled around. I decided to sober up, because I remembered what happened if you jiggled him too much. I also knew we couldn't let the children chomp chocolate all day long. When the wild animals finished feeding and started to get so restless they were breaking right out of their cages, I offered to take them for a walk on the common.

Clive's mum said she thought this was a wonderful idea but she didn't see how I could manage all the babies by myself. I suggested putting the two littlest in the double buggy and tying Vincent and Gemma with chocolate-box ribbon like a lead. Clive's mum still looked doubtful, but then Clive's granny came into the shop to see how she was coping.

'I'll take little Clive off your hands for an hour or so,' she offered.

'We could all go for a walk together,' I suggested.

'Oh no, dear, I don't think that's a good idea,' said Clive's granny quickly, but she wasn't quick enough.

'Let's go for a walk,' said Gemma, holding out her sticky hand.

'Me want to go for a run,' said Vincent, already at the door.

'Walk! Run!' Sara insisted.

Clive joined in the general uproar, telling his granny that he wanted his friends to go with him.

She was stuck with us. She didn't really *do* anything. She just pushed the buggy while I kept tight hold of Gemma and Vincent, and then when we got to the common she sat on a bench with Clive perched on her knee.

'You're free for a bit, wild animals,' I said, letting them go.

Gemma growled her way through the jungly bushes. Vincent galloped over the plain. Sara stalked prey in the undergrowth. They made a lot of wild animal noises. So did Clive. His granny bounced him up and down on her knee. She bounced him a bit too vigorously. I helped her mop him up. Then I rounded up all my wild animals. That took quite a time. I had to wrestle with them before they would submit. But at last I got them all reasonably tamed and we trailed back to the shop.

Clive's gran said she was exhausted and she'd have to go home for a lie down. Clive's mum and I had a little giggle about her after she'd gone. Then we gave the littlest wild animal his bottle, and fed the others on Marmite sandwiches and crisps and carrots and orange juice. They'd already had more than enough chocolate.

I still felt I hadn't had quite enough chocolate. I hadn't rudely grabbed for myself like the little kids, and the chocolate liqueur had come as a bit of a disappointment. I thought about this rather wistfully as I helped change and pot the wild animals (not yet properly house-trained) and then settled them down in their cardboard cages for a nap. All that running wild seemed to have tired them out. They were all fast asleep within five minutes.

I tiptoed out of the stock-room to join Clive's mum. There was a chocolate heart waiting for me on the counter. It had a special message in swirly pink icing: *Thank you, Sadie!*

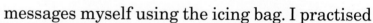

I said a lot of thank-yous back and ate it all up. It tasted wonderful.

Clive's mum showed me how to write swirly

messages myself using the icing bag. I practised on a paper bag at first because my writing went a bit haywire, but when I'd got the knack she let me write my own message on a heart: *Get well soon, Mum.*

'Ah, that's lovely,' said Clive's mum. 'Yes, I think we're all wishing that, Sadie.'

☆ SATURDAY ☆

My chocolate heart worked. Mum is very nearly better. Nan's getting better too and says she'll be back to help Mum on Monday. When I told her how I'd been mum-minding she said I was a Little Treasure. Grandad said I was too. He says he's still feeling poorly. Nan says he just wants to lie back in bed and be waited on hand and foot, and he isn't half getting on her nerves.

Mum and I are getting on just great. Saturdays are good anyway because the dads take over the babies. Our dad doesn't often come for Sara and me, but that doesn't matter. Us girls stick together.

We all had a bit of a lie in and then I got up and made tea and toast, and Sara and I got in Mum's bed and we had breakfast together. It got a bit crumby but it was very cosy all the same.

Then I got Sara sorted out and put her in her playpen.

Then I got Mum sorted out too. I poured lots of bubbles in the bath and she lay back in it like a film star and then I helped her wash her hair. We played hairdressers after, and I did her hair in all different daft styles, and then Sara wanted to join in, even though she's just got these little feathery curls that stick straight up in the air. Clive's mum had given me some of the chocolate-box ribbon so I tied a blue bow round Sara's biggest curl, and she chuckled when she saw herself in the mirror.

Then Mum brushed her hair out into her own proper style and got dressed and put some powder on her poor sore nose so that it didn't look so red.

'There! I look a new woman,' said Mum. 'I think I'm up to a little outing.'

We went down to the shopping centre, the three of us. I made Mum wrap up really warm with an extra jumper and a scarf. We had a morning coffee together, with Danish pastries, one each. Sara just sucked the jam off hers but she enjoyed it a lot, so it wasn't wasted. She was quite happy swinging her legs in the roomy buggy and

licking her lips while Mum and I sat and chatted like grown-up ladies. Then we went round the shops for a bit, looking at all the toys and clothes and choosing what we'd buy if we had all the money in the world. But then Mum got a bit tired so we caught the bus home.

I put Sara down for her nap.

I put Mum down for a nap and all. Then I did a bit of tidying and swept the floor and stuffed some things in the washing machine. A woman's work is never done. Ha ha.

Mum was ever so pleased when she woke up. She gave me the rest of her *Get Well Soon, Mum* chocolate heart. She'd only had two bites. She still hasn't got her appetite back, but she really is practically better. She says I've been the best mum-minder in the whole world.

Mum did the ironing herself this evening because I get things a bit scrumpled when I have a go. But I put Sara to bed. I read her *Dominic the Vole*. Some of the words are missing where she's had another savage gnaw, but it doesn't matter. I have read *Dominic the Vole* at least one hundred times and I know it off by heart.

Then when Sara was settled, I read to Mum while she ironed. I read her this holiday diary and she didn't half laugh.

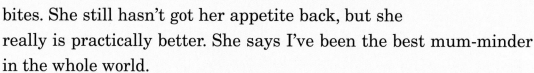

☆ SUNDAY ☆

This isn't just a holiday diary. It's a huge great blockbusting *book*. I ought to get a gold star for extra effort at the very least (hint hint). Maybe I ought to be a writer when I grow up. Though I think I'd sooner have my own chocolate shop. I'd still like to be a policewoman

too. And you get lots of money if you work in an office, so that you can buy ten or twenty ice-creams on the trot without fussing. But I know one thing. I'm never going to be a childminder.

I've done enough of that to last me six centuries.

I've finished being a mum-minder too. My mum's completely better.

She took Sara and me to the Leisure Centre this afternoon. It was absolutely great. Rachel from up the road was there too, and we went in the big pool and splashed in the fountains and screamed non-stop when they switched the big wave on. Mum went in the baby's pool with Sara. Sara splashed and screamed a lot too, and kicked her fat little feet about. I played with her for a bit while Mum had a swim. I swooped her up and down so she had her own little wave. She didn't half like that.

But after a bit she started to get shivery. So did I. So we all got out and Mum wrapped us both in big towels and then when we were dry and dressed we went and had a hot chocolate in the cafe. (Sara just had a teaspoon of froth off the top.)

Funny though. I still couldn't get properly warm. Sara started sneezing on the way home.

'Oh no,' said Mum. 'Don't say Sara's got my flu. Poor little poppet.' Then I sneezed six times without stopping.

'Oh no,' said Mum again.

'Oh yes,' I said. 'Poor little Sadie!'

'Poor little me,' said Mum. 'It looks like I'm going to have my hands full nursing you two.'

'Let's hope Gemma and Vincent and baby Clive haven't caught it too. Then it won't just be your hands you'll have two arms and a leg full as well,' I said.

Later

I am still sneezing. I am still shivery. My head hurts. I do not feel very well at all. I think I definitely do have flu. I am not pleased. Although wait a minute. If I've got flu I won't be able to go back to school tomorrow. So I'll have more holiday, even though it looks like I'll be stuck in bed.

Later still

If I don't go back to school tomorrow I won't be able to hand in my holiday diary. So what does that mean? I've filled up all this great long book for nothing!

THE CAT MUMMY

To Nancy (who loves cats)

☆ CHAPTER ONE ☆

Mabel

Do you have any pets? My best friend Sophie has got four kittens called Sporty, Scary, Baby and Posh. My second-best friend Laura has a golden Labrador dog called Dustbin. My sort-of-boyfriend Aaron has got a dog too, a black mongrel called Liquorice Allsorts, though he gets called Licky for short. My worst enemy Moyra has got a boa constrictor snake called Crusher. Well, she says she has. I've never been to her house so I don't know if she's telling fibs.

I think Sophie is ever so lucky. I love going round to her house to play with her kittens. They're so sweet, the way they scamper around

everywhere. Sophie's mum gets cross sometimes because they knock things over and they've pulled off all the curtain cords but the kittens don't care a bit when she wags her finger at them. The only thing they're the slightest bit frightened of is a little clockwork frog. They used to run away from it but now Scary is getting quite bold and dares stretch out a paw to try to catch it. I could play with Sophie's kittens all day long.

I've been to tea at Laura's house too and made friends with Dustbin. He's a cream dog with big dark shiny eyes and if you hold out your hand he'll shake paws with you. I know exactly why he's called Dustbin. He eats all the time! He's meant to be on a diet as he's getting very plump but he's forever on the scrounge. He especially likes crisps. He even licks out the bag.

Aaron's dog Licky is great at licking too. Aaron takes Licky up to the park after school. My gran and Aaron's mum sit on the bench and have a good gossip and play with Aaron's little sister Aimee and we take Licky for a run.

Then we go on the roundabout and Licky sits on Aaron's lap and

barks like crazy because he's having so much fun. Then sometimes if we nag and plead enough my gran or Aaron's mum will buy us a whippy ice-cream from the van at the park gate. Aaron always shares his ice-cream with Licky. It's not really fair on Aaron so I tried sharing my cone with Licky too, but Gran stopped me. She whispered that I mustn't, because of dog germs. My gran has a bit of a germ fixation. She's not very keen on pets. Apart from Mabel.

I don't know what she'd make of Moyra's pet snake, Crusher. I don't know what *I'd* make of Crusher either. I'm not that keen on snakes actually. Moyra sits behind me at school and today she leant forwards and shot out her arm and wrapped it right round my neck and whispered, 'Watch out, Verity, here comes Crusher!'

I *knew* it was only Moyra, and I'm pretty certain Crusher doesn't even exist – but I still screamed. Everyone giggled. Moyra practically wet herself she laughed so much. Miss Smith didn't tell me off for screaming. She didn't tell Moyra off either. She just raised her lovely black eyebrows and said, 'Settle down, girls.'

I love Miss Smith. She's a new teacher, the nicest we've ever had. I hate Moyra. If there really is a Crusher I hope he wakes up one morning and takes a good look at Moyra's beady eyes and twitchy nose, mistakes her for a giant mouse, and GOBBLES HER UP.

I certainly wouldn't want a snake for a pet, but at least it would be something exciting to boast about.

I have a pet. She is a tabby cat called Mabel. I love her dearly. But she is very, very, very *boring*. She doesn't do anything. She just sleeps. Sometimes I leave her curled up on my bed when I go to school and when I come home there she still is, in exactly the same position.

She doesn't go out at night and run round having wild encounters with big bad tom cats. Not my Mabel.

She stays indoors, dozes all evening, and then sleeps all night, back on my bed. She likes to lie on my feet like a live hot-water bottle. She's about as playful as a hot-water bottle too. I can't believe she was ever a cute little kitten like Sporty, Scary, Baby and Posh. You could run a clockwork frog right *over* Mabel and she wouldn't budge. She's never stalked or killed anything in her life. She doesn't know that's the way cats are supposed to hunt food. She is happy to amble into the kitchen and wait for Gran to open her tin of Whiskas. It's the only exercise she takes all day.

Gran says I've got to remember Mabel is very, very old. Mabel has been very, very old ever since I can remember. She was my mum's cat.

I haven't got a mum. She died the day I was born. That's almost all I know. Gran still can't talk about Mum without her eyes going watery. Even *Grandad* cries. So I don't talk about my mum because I don't want to upset them.

I've got a dad but I don't see him all that often because he's left for work before I get up and he's nearly always still at work when I go to bed. I once heard Gran say my dad is married to his job. Just so long as he doesn't marry a real lady. I definitely don't want a stepmother.

I've read all about stepmothers in fairy stories. They don't have a good image. Laura's got a step*dad* and she certainly doesn't think much of him. He's the one who put poor Dustbin on a diet. He even suggested Laura's *mum* should go on a diet and made her upset about having a big bottom – which she can't help.

Thank goodness Dad doesn't seem interested in any ladies, with big or little bottoms. He hardly ever talks about Mum but he once said she was the loveliest woman in the whole world and no-one could ever replace her. This was a great relief.

I love my dad. He sometimes takes me out

for treats on Saturdays, just him and me. For my last birthday he took me all the way on the train to Paris and Disneyland, which was fantastic – *and* he bought me a giant Minnie Mouse doll. I have her in my bed every night. It gets a bit crowded with Mabel as well.

People are sometimes sorry for me because I haven't got a mum. Sophie once put her arms round me and said it must be so awful. I was bad then and made myself look so sad that Sophie would be specially sweet to me, but I really don't mind a bit not having a mum. I don't miss her because I never knew her. The only time *I* get upset is when we go to visit my mum's grave. It's very pretty, with a white headstone, and the words *Beloved Wife and Daughter* in curly writing. Gran always arranges freesias in a little vase. They're my mum's favourite flowers. I can't help thinking about my poor mum underneath the pink and yellow flowers and the white headstone in the dark, dirty earth. There are worms. I hate thinking about my mum being buried.

I try to imagine her alive instead. I'll tell you a very private secret. I sometimes talk about my mum to Mabel, because Mabel doesn't ever get upset.

I talk and talk and talk about my mum. Mabel listens. When she's not asleep.

☆ CHAPTER TWO ☆

Where's Mabel?

When I got home from school I ran into the hall and stepped straight into this little mess of cat sick.

'Y-u-c-k!'

I was wearing open-toed sandals, which made it a *lot* worse. I hopped around going, 'Yuck Yuck Yuck' and Gran sighed and hurried me into the kitchen and got a bowl of water and a cloth and some disinfectant.

Mabel was dithering at the end of the hall, hanging her head.

'Honestly, Mabel! Why do you have to throw up right where I'm going to walk in it? What have you been eating, you naughty cat? You're disgusting!'

Mabel drooped and slunk away.

'Yes, you jolly well should be ashamed,' I said.

'Don't be too hard on Mabel, Verity,' said Gran. 'I don't think she's

very well. That's the second time she's been sick – and she's had a little accident too.'

'Mabel's always having little accidents,' I said.

She's so lazy she doesn't amble over to her litter tray in time.

'Mabel isn't getting any younger, you know,' said Gran.

'*You're* not getting any younger, Gran, but you don't sick up your food or do little wees all over the place,' I said, giggling.

'You cheeky baggage,' said Gran, pretending to give me a smack on the bottom.

She laughed, but she still looked a bit worried. My tummy clenched.

'Gran, there's nothing *seriously* wrong with Mabel, is there?' I asked. 'She has just got a little tummy upset, hasn't she?'

Gran hesitated. 'I hope so. I think she's just getting older, dear, like I said.'

'Maybe we should take her to the vet's?'

'I'm not sure there's much they can do for her.'

My tummy clenched tighter.

'But she will be all right, won't she,

Gran?' I said. 'I mean . . . she's not going to die or anything?'

I felt myself blushing as if I'd said a really rude word. We hardly ever say words like 'die' or 'death' in my family.

'Well . . .' said Gran, swallowing. 'We've all got to pass away at some time.'

'But not for ages and ages. Mabel isn't going to die *soon*, is she?'

Gran didn't answer properly. She just wriggled her shoulders. 'Shall I make some of my special home-made lemonade? And then maybe you'd like to watch television?'

Gran only makes her lemonade on special days and she usually nags me *not* to watch television. She likes me to read a book or draw a picture or play in the garden.

I started to feel panicky. Gran seemed to think that Mabel might be going to die soon. It sounds so silly but I'd never ever thought about Mabel *dying*. I knew she was old but I sort of assumed she'd stagger on for ever on her soft spreading paws.

I was starting to feel really, really mean for scolding poor Mabel. I wanted to give her a big cuddle and say sorry.

'Back in a minute, Gran,' I said, and I went charging upstairs to my bedroom, Mabel's usual lurking spot.

My bed was empty.

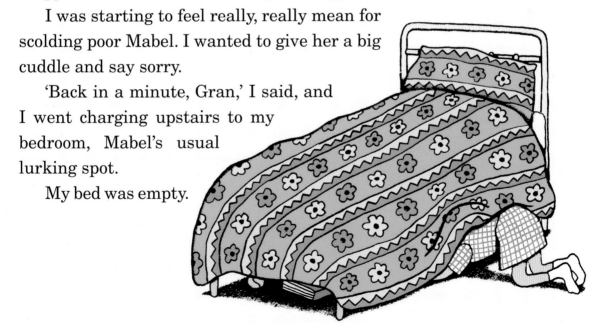

Well, Minnie Mouse was lying there with her yellow heels sticking up at an angle – but no Mabel.

'Where's Mabel?' I said, tossing Minnie onto the floor.

I looked underneath my bed. Mabel might be really embarrassed about being sick on the hall carpet. She'd hidden underneath my bed in the past. But she wasn't there now.

'Mabel?' I called. 'Where are you, Mabel?'

I looked all round my bedroom. I searched through the toys and clothes on the carpet. I looked on the windowsill behind the curtain. There was no sign of her anywhere.

I went to look in Gran and Grandad's bedroom. Though Gran always kept their door shut to stop Mabel exploring, Mabel had long ago learnt the knack of nudging it sharply with her hip so that the catch sprang open. I looked on the bed, the rug, the rocking chair, even under the dressing table.

I looked in the bathroom although Mabel detests water and shrieks if I splash her when she noses in and I'm having a bath.

I went charging downstairs and into the kitchen. Gran was stirring her lemonade.

'Gran, I can't find Mabel!'

'She's not on your bed? Though I must say it's not a very hygienic habit, especially if Mabel's poorly. We don't want her being sick on your bed now, do we?'

I wanted Mabel so badly I wouldn't have cared.

'Where *is* she, Gran?'

'What about the living room?'

One of Mabel's favourite snoozing places is the rug in front of the fire. The fire isn't on during the summer but Mabel doesn't seem to notice. She lies there as if she's toasting herself, first lying on one side, then after a little yawn and stretch, settling down to give the other side a turn. I sometimes sit on the chair by the fire and gently rest my bare feet on Mabel's back. She feels like my big furry slipper.

But she wasn't on the rug, though there were cat hairs in a Mabel shape to show she'd had a little lie-down since Gran vacuumed this morning. Mabel wasn't in the chairs or on the sofa or under the table. She wasn't anywhere at all.

'Gran, I can't find her!'

'Mabel?' Gran called. 'Puss puss puss! Come on, old lady. Ma-bel!'

Mabel didn't come.

'I wonder if she's in the garden?' said Gran. 'Here's your lemonade anyway, Verity. And a chockie bickie.'

Gran is the loveliest gran ever, but like all grans she often treats me like a baby. Chockie bickie! That's the way you talk to really *little* kids.

I ate the chocolate biscuit in two bites, drained the lemonade in the glass, and then dashed off to search the garden for Mabel.

She can get out from her cat flap in the back door, but recently she's stayed indoors. She had a worrying encounter with another cat who pounced on her. It was the big ginger tom from up the road. He didn't really do her any harm and I managed to chase him away, but Mabel went all quivery for ages afterwards. She hasn't set one paw in the garden since.

I still searched it high and low. Grandad searched it too when he came home. Then he said he'd have a look round all the streets for her.

'I want to go with you, Grandad,' I said. Gran and Grandad didn't think this a good idea. They wouldn't say why at first. I pestered them.

'Something sad might have happened to Mabel, darling,' Gran said eventually. 'We wouldn't want you to see and be upset.'

'What sort of something?' I asked – though I knew.

'Mabel might have been run over, dear. She's getting very old and slow, and I don't think she can see too well,' said Gran.

'But I need to help Grandad look for her! What if she *has* been hurt? I can't stand thinking of Mabel in pain, all lost and frightened.'

'Grandad will do his best to find her, Verity,' said Gran.

But Grandad came back home shaking his head. There was still no sign of Mabel anywhere.

'I want her so much!' I said, and I started to cry.

This time I was glad Gran treats me like a baby. She sat me on her lap and rocked me and Grandad read me a story. I stopped crying – but it didn't stop me aching for Mabel.

I was still wide awake when Dad came home from work. He put his head round my bedroom door, and then sat on my bed while I had another cry.

'What's happened to Mabel, Dad? She can't have disappeared. She never goes wandering off. Not far, anyway. She isn't anywhere. I've searched and searched.'

'I know, pet. Look, we'll write out a notice about Mabel being missing. I'll do lots of copies on my computer and we'll pin them up all over the neighbourhood.'

'And will we get her back then?'

'I hope so, darling.'

'Do you promise?'

Dad hesitated. 'You know I can't promise, Verity.'

'I want Mabel so much, Dad. I haven't been very nice to her recently. I've moaned at her for being so sleepy and yet I know she can't help it. I'd give anything to have her sleeping here on my bed right now.'

'I know, love.'

'I keep thinking about her. She's maybe crying too . . .'

Dad stayed with me for ages, trying to calm me down. I think I went to sleep for a bit. But then I woke up alone in the dark and I felt for Mabel – and she wasn't there.

I hugged Minnie Mouse instead but she wasn't the same. Nothing could ever replace Mabel. I wished I could hold her in my arms and tell her just how much she meant to me.

☆ CHAPTER THREE ☆

The Ancient Egyptian Cats

I didn't sleep properly that night. Mabel padded in and out of my dreams and whenever I woke up the bed was so cold and empty without her.

I had another search of the house when I got up.

'I've had a good look myself,' said Gran. 'There's no sign of her.'

'Let's open her tin of Whiskas and bang the tin opener about a bit. That *always* makes her come,' I said desperately.

Gran opened the tin. She banged the tin opener lots of times. So did I. We both called for Mabel. But Mabel didn't come.

Grandad had another good look when he went to get the newspapers. No luck.

'Perhaps she's been kidnapped!' I said.

'Darling, nobody would want an old cat like Mabel,' said Gran.

'*I* want her,' I said, and I cried again.

I cried so much that Gran and Grandad got really worried.

'Do try and stop, Verity. You'll make yourself ill,' said Gran. 'Come on, now, you're going to be late for school.'

'Maybe she's not in a fit state for school?' said Grandad.

'No, I'm not in a fit state at all,' I sobbed, hoping that I'd be able to stay off and search for Mabel.

But Gran was firm. I had to go to school no matter what. She stuck the cleaned sandals on my feet and fetched me a clean school dress from the airer.

'Come on, stop that crying now, Verity,' she said, buttoning me into my dress.

She couldn't button my lips though.

'You don't understand, Gran. Don't you *care* that Mabel's missing?'

Gran stopped buttoning.

'I care a great deal,' she said, and her voice suddenly sounded wavery, like a radio not tuned in properly. 'I've known Mabel much longer than you, Verity. I remember when we first got her as a kitten and your mother—' Gran's voice suddenly stopped. There were tears in her eyes.

My tummy clenched so tight I couldn't talk either, but I squeezed Gran's hand to show her I was sorry.

'I'll take you to school today, Verity,' said Grandad. 'Come on, dear. Leave your gran be for now.'

Gran wasn't making any sound but the tears were running down her cheeks. Silent crying seems more frightening than noisy sobs. I hurried off to school with Grandad, looking in every single garden on the way. I kept stopping to peer underneath cars too just in case Mabel was curled up anywhere.

Grandad gave me a hug at the school gate.

'How about a big smile for Grandad?' he asked. I couldn't even manage a very little smile. Grandad was finding it hard to smile too.

'I *wish* I didn't have to go to school, Grandad,' I said, wondering if he'd weaken and let me go back home with him.

But Grandad said maybe playing with my friends would take my mind off Mabel. I didn't see how he could say that. My mind was going Mabel-Mabel-Mabel like a burglar alarm and when I went into the classroom and started talking to Sophie and Laura and Aaron the Mabel noise didn't stop. It got louder.

'What's up, Verity?' Sophie asked, putting her arm round me.

'Mabel's missing!' I wailed, and I told her all about it.

Sophie was very comforting. She gave me half her Mars Bar from her lunch box and told me that Sporty and Scary and Baby and Posh's mother once went missing.

'She was gone for ages. She made herself a nest in the garden shed. That's where she had her kittens. Maybe your Mabel's having kittens too?'

'Mabel's much too old to have kittens.'

'Maybe she's just gone off on the scrounge,' said Laura. 'Our dog Dustbin does that. He goes into people's gardens and barks piteously as if he's starving and sometimes they fall for it and feed him.'

'I don't think Mabel would do that. She's been a bit off her food recently,' I said. 'She keeps being sick.' I put my head down on my desk. 'I was horrid to her because I stepped in it, but it wasn't her fault at all. Maybe she's really, really ill.'

'Our Licky is sick lots and lots. He eats grass, the silly boy, like he's got this mad idea he's a sheep. Does your Mabel eat grass?'

'No, she just likes her cat food,' I said, speaking into my desk.

'Good morning, everyone,' said Miss Smith cheerily, coming into the classroom. 'Verity? What's up with you, poppet? Are you sleepy?'

'Mmm,' I mumbled.

'Did you stay up late watching television?'

'No. I couldn't sleep properly.'

'Why's that?' said Miss Smith, coming up to my desk and squatting down beside me.

'I had these bad dreams.'

'Oh dear. Did you tell your mum?'

'My mum's dead,' I said, and I sniffed hard. Miss Smith looked very upset. 'I'm so sorry,' she said, as if my mum had only died yesterday.

I drooped in my desk while Miss Smith started the lesson, telling us all this stuff about the Ancient Egyptians. We're doing them this term.

Miss Smith looks a bit like an Ancient Egyptian herself with her straight black hair and her big outlined eyes. We had to do an Ancient Egyptian picture last week. You have to draw all the people looking sideways. Sophie and I got the giggles wondering if the Ancient Egyptians walked about like that.

I didn't feel at all like giggling now. Moyra gave me a little dig in the back.

'My pet snake Crusher's gone missing too,' she whispered. 'I wonder where he can have got to?'

I knew what was coming. A few seconds later Moyra's arm slithered over my shoulders.

'It's Crusher!' she hissed.

This time I didn't scream. I didn't even flinch.

Moyra tried again, her arm wrapping right round my waist, but I still didn't move.

'Moyra! Leave Verity alone, please,' said Miss Smith.

'You're no fun,' Moyra whispered.

I knew I wasn't any fun. I slumped further down in my chair, thinking about Mabel. I kept remembering how I'd shouted at her for being sick and the sad, shamed way she'd slunk off. I couldn't bear it.

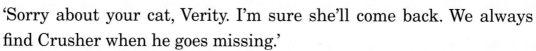

I had to find my hankie quick. I snuffled noisily. Everyone politely took no notice – until I got another poke in the back from Moyra. I thought I was under another Crusher attack, but she whispered, 'Sorry about your cat, Verity. I'm sure she'll come back. We always find Crusher when he goes missing.'

'Moyra!' said Miss Smith.

'I was just saying nice stuff about Verity's cat, Miss Smith!' said Moyra.

'She was, Miss Smith,' I said, blowing my nose.

I'm not always good, but I *am* truthful.

The whole class looked astonished. Moyra and I are famed for our deadly enmity and yet here we were sticking up for each other. Even Miss Smith looked surprised.

'Well, I'm glad to see you two being friendly for once,' she said. 'Still, we're really supposed to be thinking about the Ancient Egyptians, not cats. Though as a matter of fact the Ancient Egyptians were extremely interested in cats. They kept them as special pets and looked after them very lovingly. If an enemy soldier held a cat as a kind of living armour the Egyptian soldiers wouldn't attack because they were so worried about hurting the cat. They even had a special cat goddess called Bastet. They built a big cat cemetery in her name. When a cat died the owners would shave their eyebrows as a sign of mourning – and very special cats were even made into mummies.'

'Mummies! Wow. Tell us about mummies, Miss Smith,' said Moyra.

I stopped listening. I was saying a prayer to Bastet.

'Please let me find Mabel, oh great cat goddess Bastet,' I whispered. 'Please please please let me find Mabel.'

I had my eyes tightly shut. When I opened them Miss Smith was holding up a picture of a cat. It looked very odd, long and thin, with no tail or paws, but it had a very distinct cat face and little pointed cat ears. It seemed to be made of cloth rather than fur so I thought it was maybe a toy cat.

'This is a cat mummy,' said Miss Smith, and she told us exactly how the Ancient Egyptians made their poor dead cats into mummies. And this time I listened.

☆ CHAPTER FOUR ☆

The Mabel Mummy

The cat goddess Bastet granted my prayer – but in the worst way possible.

Gran met me from school. She had make-up on and she looked smart, but she was still sad. There was still no sign of Mabel.

'But we've got to remember she's been missing less than twenty-four hours,' said Gran.

It seemed like she'd been missing twenty-four days. No, twenty-four *weeks*. When I went indoors I wished there was some magic way I could rewind those twenty-four hours so I could step in the sick in

the hall but then pick Mabel up and cuddle her close and tell her how sorry I was that she wasn't feeling well.

But the carpet was clean this time. There was no Mabel hanging her head in the hall.

'I'll make us a little snack,' said Gran, though neither of us was feeling hungry.

I went trailing upstairs to my bedroom.

Minnie was sprawled on my bed. I flopped down beside her for a minute. I kicked off my sandals and curled up as if I was going to sleep. Gran came to find me after five minutes.

'Are you having a little nap, Verity? That's a good idea. I'll call you later on for tea, all right?' Gran tiptoed away. I kept my eyes shut but I couldn't sleep. I felt cold and shivery even though it was a hot day. I didn't want to get right under the covers in my school dress. I suddenly wanted my cosy old winter dressing gown. It was made of blue furry stuff and it had a big black cat head on both pockets.

I got up off the bed and searched through my wardrobe but I couldn't find it at first. It had slipped off the hanger and fallen onto my shoes. I knelt down and rummaged for it. I felt fur . . . real fur.

I gave a little gasp and pulled it out carefully, holding my breath. Mabel was nestled up inside my dressing gown. But there was something terribly wrong with her. Her eyes were half open and she seemed very very stiff.

'Mabel,' I whispered. I shook her gently to try to wake her up. But she couldn't wake up now. My poor darling Mabel was dead.

'Oh Mabel,' I said, and I cradled her in my arms and rocked her to and fro.

I wanted to cry out to Gran but I was so choked up I could barely make a sound. I thought about what would happen next. Mabel would be buried. I couldn't bear the idea of her being smothered under all that dirty earth. Mabel didn't like it out in the garden any more. She'd be so frightened and lonely. And then the worms would get her . . .

'No!' I whispered. 'I'm not going to let them bury you, Mabel, I promise. I'll look after you. I'll keep you safe.'

But I couldn't just leave her tucked up in my dressing gown. She was already starting to look and feel and smell a little strange. I wasn't quite sure how things might progress, but I knew it wouldn't be pleasant. I had to find some way of preserving Mabel.

Then it came to me. It was as if the great cat goddess Bastet had put her holy paw upon me to give me the idea. I would make Mabel into a mummy! I wouldn't tell Gran or Grandad or Dad. I knew they might find it too weird – and Gran would probably fuss about hygiene.

I had to do it. It was the perfect way of preserving Mabel for ever. Then I could still hold her in my arms and tell her I loved her and whisper messages to my mum. Mabel would be just like a toy cat, able to stay with me for ever and ever and ever.

So . . . I had to get cracking and turn her into a mummy while Gran thought I was having a nap. I knew the Ancient Egyptians had taken seventy days but I had less than seventy *minutes*.

I carefully opened up my old dressing gown and spread it out on the bedroom floor. Mabel lay rigidly in the middle. She didn't look well at all. I tried to smooth her fur and mopped her up carefully with a little wad of tissues.

When she was as clean and tidy as I could get her I squatted on my heels, thinking about the next step. I knew what it was. You had to take a piece of wire and stick it in the head and hook out the brain.

Mabel's half-open eyes looked at me. I knew I couldn't possibly do any hooking. I decided to wrap her up whole. I was worried that all her insides might go bad. I had to preserve Mabel under her mummy wrappings.

I knew what the Ancient Egyptians used. It was natron, a special kind of salt. I didn't think you could get natron now. I'd never seen it on the shelves in Sainsbury's. I didn't think ordinary Saxa salt was the right sort of stuff. Then I remembered the big jar of lavender bath salts on the bathroom shelf.

I thought they would be ideal. I crept to the bathroom to check. I saw on the label that they included preservative. Great! Plus they were so sweet-smelling they'd keep Mabel as fragrant as a flower.

I stole back to my bedroom with the jar and tipped the entire contents over Mabel. It looked as if she'd been caught in a lavender snowstorm.

'There, darling,' I whispered, brushing the salts out of her eyes so we could look at each other one last time. 'Now, we'll make you into a mummy.'

Gran kept old sheets at the top of her airing cupboard and only ever got them out when she had to make me a costume for a school play, or when Sophie and I wanted to play ghosts. I took a big sheet and then got cracking with my scissors. I couldn't just wrap the sheet round Mabel like a parcel. I knew you had to make bandages and wrap and wrap and wrap very tightly in a special pattern.

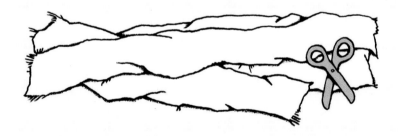

I tried to cut the sheet into neat strips. It was very difficult because I didn't have any decent scissors, just the old blunt-edged ones I used for my scrapbook. Gran had special sharp scissors in the kitchen but I couldn't risk creeping downstairs. I struggled on as best I could with my own stupid baby scissors until my hands ached, and then I tried ripping bits of sheet.

Time was getting on. I decided I'd better start wrapping with the scraps of sheet I already had. I picked Mabel up tenderly and tried to get her into the right position. I knew I had to straighten her paws and tail so that she would look like a long-necked cat doll when she was finished.

Mabel wouldn't straighten up. She curled up with her paws out and her tail wrapped round herself in her usual going-to-sleep position. She simply wouldn't budge from it. I tried tugging hard but I was terrified her poor old legs might actually snap, and I didn't dare try her tail because it was already so thin and threadbare.

I had no idea how the Ancient Egyptians solved this problem. I decided I simply had to make the best of it and wrapped Mabel up with her paws sticking out and her back all bunched. It wasn't easy. I've never been much good at wrapping Christmas presents. I can't even stick strips of sheet with Sellotape. Every time I got a bit round one part of Mabel another part unravelled. I had to keep tying big knots. Mabel started to look like the most untidy parcel in the world.

I was nearly in tears because I so wanted her to look beautiful and dignified. But as I went on wrapping and wrapping I was able to disguise her shape more – and I was starting to get the hang of doing it neatly. It was like the first time I tried to put my hair into a plait at the back and it was all lopsided and half the hair hung down, but now I've done it so many times my fingers flash in and out and it ends up as neat as ninepence.

Mabel didn't end up quite as neat as that. As tidy as twopence, more like. But at least she was now officially a mummy.

I got my best set of felt tips and carefully inked green eyes and a pink nose and a red smiley mouth on the sheet over her head. Then I tried to do Egyptian symbols all round her sheeted body. I did that open eye of Horos to protect her and the Ankh sign for good luck. Then I drew lots of things that Mabel liked, a can of cat food and the hearthrug and my bed, with a border of mice and fish and birds to finish it off.

I sat back on my heels when I'd finished and admired Mabel. I needed to keep her in a sarcophagus, the special mummy case. I couldn't think what to use. I tried a shoe box but it wasn't big enough, and it was the wrong shape. I needed something biggish because Mabel was pretty bulky now.

I decided my old duffle bag that I use for swimming might just do as a temporary measure, so I eased Mabel into it as carefully as I could. I put my head in the top of the bag and kissed her wrappings and told her I loved her for ever and ever and ever. Then I gently and reverently placed her in the back of my wardrobe. It wasn't pyramid shape but it was dark and private, so it made a reasonable tomb.

☆ CHAPTER FIVE ☆

Nightmare

'Your little nap did you good, darling,' said Gran, when I went downstairs for tea. 'Mmm! You smell very fresh and pretty!'

'You've got a bit of colour back in your cheeks, poppet,' said Grandad.

They both looked pale and tired but they were trying hard to smile and be cheerful. Gran served us sausage and mash, our favourite – but nobody cleared their plate.

I kept peering at Mabel's dish in the corner of the kitchen. She always had her tea while we ate ours. Sometimes she came scavenging for my leftovers. She particularly liked mashed potato. I had to be careful though. If I gave her too much she was sick.

I thought about the last time poor Mabel was sick and how mean I'd been. My mashed potato got stuck in my throat and I was very nearly sick myself.

Grandad's hand reached out and patted mine. Gran took my plate away and gave me another drink.

'Your dad's going to do his best to come home early tonight,' said Gran.

I wasn't too sure about this. Dad always had to work very, very late. But today he came home just as Gran was clearing the table.

'I'll get your own tea, dear,' she said.

'I'll have it later,' said Dad. 'I thought Verity and I would go out first. I've got heaps of posters about Mabel. We'll pin them up over the neighbourhood. I've even used a photo of her, look, Verity.'

I looked. Dad had done a wonderful poster with a big blown-up picture of Mabel curled up asleep, under the heading HAVE YOU SEEN OUR CAT MABEL?

My heart started banging so hard I thought it was going to bounce right through my chest and make a mess of my school dress. Dad and I trudged down street after street after street. We pinned Mabel's poster to trees and fences and lamp-posts everywhere we went.

'Don't worry, Verity, we'll find Mabel now,' said Dad, taking hold of my hand. 'Someone's bound to see the poster and recognize Mabel and ring our number. She can't have vanished into thin air.'

My heart went bang bang bang. I knew I should tell Dad that Mabel wasn't missing. He had done a hundred posters asking if anyone had seen her. There was only one person in the whole world who knew exactly where she was, entombed in my wardrobe.

I wondered if Dad would understand? I didn't dare risk telling him. You couldn't talk about things like death to Dad. It made him think about Mum. I remembered Gran this morning. It would be even worse if *Dad* started crying.

So I didn't say anything. I was very, very quiet all the way round the neighbourhood and I was very, very quiet when we got home. We were *all* very, very quiet.

I was glad when Gran sent me up to bed. I lay there wide awake. I waited until I heard Gran and Grandad go up to bed. I waited even longer, until I heard Dad go up to bed too. It was a good job I waited, because Dad crept into my room. I closed my eyes tight and lay very still. Dad stood beside my bed a long time. Then he sighed, gently tucked the covers up under my chin, and went out the room.

I still had to wait ages and ages, just to be safe. But when there hadn't been any sound in the house for a long, long time I crept out of bed and very slowly and cautiously opened my wardrobe door. There was a strange smell, half sweet, half sour – bath salts mixed up with the new worrying smell of Mabel.

I decided I mustn't let this put me off. Mabel couldn't help it after all.

I reached into the back of the wardrobe and reverently pulled out the duffle bag. I tried hard but I couldn't pull the Mabel mummy out. I couldn't really see what I was doing in the dark. I had to content myself with inserting one hand into the bag and stroking Mabel's bandages. It was very soothing, very, very soothing . . .

I woke up in the middle of the night to find myself huddled against the wardrobe, the duffle bag clasped to my chest. I wanted to take it back to bed with me, but I didn't dare risk it. I put Mabel back in the wardrobe, shut the door, and then crawled back into bed. I was freezing cold so I wrapped the duvet tightly round me.

I think it was the duvet that gave me the nightmare. I was dead and someone was trying to hook my brains out and I screamed and then they were wrapping me up in bandages, tighter and tighter, and I screamed again. I screamed for someone to come and help me because I was being turned into a mummy . . .

'Verity! Verity, darling, it's Dad. I'm here. Wake up! You're having a nightmare.'

I started sobbing, still thrashing my arms and legs around to free them from the mummy bandages. The duvet fell away and the only thing holding me tightly was Dad.

'Oh, Dad,' I sobbed.

He held me close.

'What's up?' Gran said sleepily, out on the landing. 'Is Verity crying?'

'She had a bad dream,' said Dad. 'She was shouting.'

'What was I shouting?' I said, suddenly scared. 'Did I shout about Mabel?'

Dad didn't answer until Gran had shuffled back to bed.

'I couldn't quite make out what you were saying, pet, but you seemed to be calling for . . . for Mummy.'

I didn't know what to say. My heart was banging again. Dad cleared his throat as if he was about to say more, but no words came out.

There was a deep silence in the dark room.

☆ CHAPTER SIX ☆

Mabel, the Spirit of the Dead

We all overslept in the morning. It was just as well. Gran noticed all the bath salts were missing.

'How can they have disappeared?' Gran said, bewildered.

She asked Grandad if he'd used them. He said he didn't want to smell like a lavender bush, thanks very much, so he never used so much as a sprinkle.

'Verity? *You* didn't use them all up, did you?' said Gran. 'I know it can't have been your dad. He only ever has a quick shower.'

'I – I might have used some of them,' I mumbled, running away from Gran into my bedroom. 'Sorry, Gran, I've got to pack my school bag.'

But Gran followed me into my bedroom. She sniffed suspiciously.

'My goodness! I can *smell* the bath salts! What on earth did you do? Tip the whole *jar* in your bath?'

'Please don't be cross, Gran,' I said, frantically shoving my books and PE kit into my school bag.

I shoved a little *too* frantically and the zip jammed. I tugged. I tugged too hard.

'Oh no!'

'Verity! Silly girl! You should have eased the zip. Now look at it! Where's your duffle bag? You'd better take your stuff in that.'

'No! No, I . . . I can't. I don't like my duffle bag. No-one takes duffle bags to school any more. This bag's still fine, Gran. I'll pin it. Oh please, let's hurry, we're *late*.'

I dodged round Gran, clutching my broken bag in my arms. I hoped she'd have forgotten all about the bath salts by the time school was over.

We couldn't forget about poor Mabel. There were all the posters on every tree and fence, her sweet face peering at us plaintively.

'I'd give anything in the whole world for Mabel to be safe and sound somewhere,' Gran muttered. 'I'll stay in all day just in case anyone phones with news of her.'

'Oh Gran,' I said.

I trailed into school, feeling terrible. The bell had already gone but Miss Smith didn't tell me off when I sidled into the classroom.

'How are you today, Verity? Any more bad dreams?' she asked.

I nodded. 'Horrible nightmares.'

'Oh dear,' she said, and she patted my shoulder as I went past.

Sophie and Laura and Aaron were all extra-nice to me. Even *Moyra* was nice. She offered to share her sweets with me at break-time. She had two big wiggly green jelly snakes.

'You can have one if you want, Verity,' she said.

I said I wasn't very hungry, thank you. She did tease a bit then, shaking a snake right in my face and asking if I was frightened of *sweets* – but Aaron elbowed her out the way and asked if I was going to the swings after school. Laura told me her  next-door neighbour had heard a cat mewing in the night and it might have been Mabel. Sophie said if Mabel didn't ever come back maybe I'd like Sporty or Scary or Baby or Posh because her mum said they couldn't keep all the kittens.

I thanked Aaron but said I didn't really feel like a trip to the swings. I thanked Laura and said I didn't think it could have been Mabel. I thanked Sophie and said I loved Sporty and Scary and Baby and Posh . . . but they could never ever replace my Mabel.

I thought about Mabel most of the morning.

I got a lot of my sums wrong. But after dinner Miss Smith gave another lesson on the Ancient Egyptians, and I started to listen properly. She held up this rather scary-looking jackal mask and asked who wanted to try it on and be Anubis, the god of the dead. Moyra nearly wet herself she was so desperate to be chosen. Miss

Smith let everyone take turns while she told us all about the Ancient Egyptians' beliefs about death.

They were sure the spirit left the body but might come back to it later on. That's why they thought it very important to preserve the bodies. They needed to be kept in spic and span condition in case the spirit paid a visit.

I felt relieved that I had done my very best for Mabel. I decided to leave the wardrobe door ajar so that Mabel's spirit could waft out and go for a walk round all her old haunts whenever she felt like it.

'Can you see the spirit, Miss Smith?' I asked.

'Well, the Ancient Egyptians painted pictures of the spirits of the dead, and they always drew them like big birds.'

I blinked at the idea, trying to imagine Mabel with wings. She'd look a little odd but I knew she'd enjoy being able to fly. She could swoop straight out the house and up over the rooftops and save her poor old paws. She could have such fun chasing all the sparrows and perch in the tallest tree and never ever get stuck.

Miss Smith showed us all a picture of Anubis weighing a heart on the scale to see if it balanced with the feather of truth so that the mummy could be made immortal.

'So the mummies live for ever and ever and you can be together in the afterlife?' I said, imagining Mabel and me flying hand in paw for ever.

Miss Smith was looking at me worriedly.

'It's just what the Ancient Egyptians believed, Verity,' she said gently.

'But we can believe it too,' I said.

'Well . . .' said Miss Smith uncertainly.

'*I* believe it,' said Moyra. 'I love the Ancient Egyptians. Show us those snaky demons in that Dead Book, Miss Smith. They're brilliant!'

Miss Smith started to tell everyone about the serpent demons and the crocodile monsters. Everyone got very excited. I didn't join in. I thought about Mabel instead.

I decided I needed to fill her wardrobe tomb with some special toys and a tin or two of Whiskas. She once had her own catnip mouse but it had got lost somewhere. I didn't have any other sort of mice, apart from Minnie, and she was much too big.

At the end of lessons Miss Smith called me back.

'Verity? Can I have a little word?'

I thought she was going to tell me off for not paying attention. I got flustered and forgot about the broken zip on my school bag. Everything fell out with a thump and a clatter as I made my way up to Miss Smith's desk.

'Oh dear,' said Miss Smith. She helped me collect up my stuff. 'It's not your day today, is it, Verity?'

'No, Miss Smith.'

'Verity . . . you seem rather unhappy at the moment,' Miss Smith said gently.

I hung my head.

'And you're obviously not sleeping very well.'

'I'm sorry, Miss Smith.'

'It's not your fault, poppet. I'm not telling you off. I just want to try to help.' She paused.

'I know things must be very sad at home at the moment.'

I looked up. Someone must have told her about Mabel.

'Perhaps . . . perhaps you could try talking about your mum with your dad? Or maybe your gran?'

I blinked at Miss Smith, wondering why she'd suddenly switched to talking about my *mum*?

'I can't talk about my mum,' I said. My throat went tight because the only person I could ever talk to about Mum was Mabel.

'Can I go now, Miss Smith?' I whispered. I didn't want to burst into tears in front of her.

I ran off quickly before she said yes. I thought I heard her calling me, but I didn't stop.

Gran was waiting at the gate, looking anxious.

'Where have you been, Verity? Aaron and the others came out ten minutes ago. Did Miss Smith keep you in?'

'Oh, she just wanted to talk to me for a bit,' I said, hurrying along beside Gran. 'Can I have an ice-cream?'

'No, dear. And don't try to change the subject! What did she want to talk to you about?'

'Oh . . . nothing.'

Gran sighed.

'Are you in any trouble?'

'No, Gran.'

'Verity? Are you telling me the truth?'

I managed to look Gran straight in the eye.

'Yes, Gran.'

☆ CHAPTER SEVEN ☆

Mabel the Mummy

I try very hard to tell the truth. That's what my name Verity means. You look it up. It's Latin for truth.

I can be as naughty as the next person but I try not to tell lies. However . . . it was getting harder and harder with this Mabel-mummy situation. I hadn't been *completely* truthful about the missing bath salts, or my duffle bag, or my conversation with Miss Smith. But I hadn't told any actual downright lies. Yet.

As soon as I got home I went charging up to my bedroom to have a private word with Mabel. I shut my bedroom door and put a chair against it just in case. Then I opened my wardrobe.

I wished I hadn't.

The smell was a lot worse. The bath salts weren't doing their work. Mabel smelt as if she was in dreadful distress and needed cleaning up. I felt I should ease her out of the duffle bag and attend to her, but when I undid the drawstring at the top the smell was suddenly so overpowering that I reeled backwards. I shoved Mabel in her bag to the very back of the wardrobe and closed the door quick.

I sat on my heels wondering what on earth to do. I wondered and wondered and wondered.

'What are you up to, Verity?' Gran called. 'Are you having another nap?'

'No, Gran. Coming!' I said hastily and shot downstairs.

I didn't want to risk her coming up to my bedroom when the smell had seeped so strongly out of the wardrobe. The smell seemed to have stuck to me too because Gran wrinkled her nose when I went into the kitchen.

'Whatever's that awful smell, darling?'

'What smell, Gran?' I said, trying to look as wide-eyed and innocent as possible.

'Verity . . . ?' Gran paused, looking embarrassed. 'You haven't had a little accident have you?'

'No, Gran!' I said indignantly.

Gran was still looking at me very strangely.

'I think you'd better pop off and have a bath anyway, dear – and change your dress too.' Gran paused. 'I've bought some new bath salts but please be very careful with them this time. Only tip a little into your bath.'

So I had a bath and felt a lot fresher. But the clean clothes were a BIG problem. They were hanging in my wardrobe. When I opened the door a crack and smelt them I knew I couldn't possibly put any of them on.

I started to panic. I'd have to try to creep downstairs with all my clothes in the middle of the night and put them in the washing machine. But what was I going to do *now*?

I ended up putting on my old fairy costume which I found screwed up at the bottom of my toy box. I hadn't worn it for a couple of years. It was much too short and much too tight. I felt a perfect fool, but at least it only smelt of old teddy bears.

Gran looked astonished when I lumbered downstairs, wings flapping, net skirts barely covering my knickers.

'What on earth have you got that fairy frock on for, Verity?'

'I wanted to play fairies, Gran. Please let me,' I said, and I swooped about, pretending to be a soppy little fairy.

'What a lovely fairy! Can I have a wish?' said Grandad, coming in from the garden.

I had to keep on and on playing

fairies. I was still flitting about granting magic wishes when Dad came home – early again, in time for tea.

'Is that the latest fashion?' Dad said warily, peering at me.

'Oh Dad, don't be silly,' I said. 'I'm being a fairy, right?'

I did a daft pointy-toe dance to demonstrate.

Dad and Gran and Grandad had a muttered conference while I twirled.

'She seems to have perked up astonishingly.'

'She didn't even ask if there were any phone calls about Mabel.'

'I came home early in case she wanted to do another search of the neighbourhood, but it seems a shame to suggest it now.'

It was easier if they all thought me a heartless baby who'd forgotten all about Mabel, but I hated having to act the part, especially when Gran pandered to me and gave me an extra fairy cake at tea.

We were all still sitting at the table when the doorbell rang. Gran went to answer it and came back into the living room . . . with Miss Smith!

'I'm so sorry! I've interrupted you when you're having your meal,' said Miss Smith.

'Not at all! We've finished anyway. Let me get you a cup of tea or coffee, Miss Smith,' said Dad, leaping up.

'I'll do it, dear,' said Gran. She doesn't like anyone helping her in the kitchen.

Grandad was looking at me, eyebrows raised.

'Is our Verity in a spot of bother at school, Miss Smith?' he asked. Gran frowned.

'Verity? What have you been up to? Go and put a clean school frock on, dear. Whatever will Miss Smith think seeing you in your funny fairy outfit?'

'Oh no, please. You look sweet, Verity,' said Miss Smith. 'Don't worry, Verity's not in any trouble at all. I just came round because Verity dropped her purse. It fell out of her school bag and rolled under a desk. I brought it round in case you were worried about it.'

'How kind of you,' said Dad. 'Say thank you, Verity.'

'I knew it was silly taking that broken bag to school. You'll take your duffle bag tomorrow,' said Gran.

'I can't!'

They all looked at me.

'I mean . . . I lost my duffle bag.'

'Don't be silly, Verity, of course you haven't lost it,' said Gran. 'And *do* go and put some decent clothes on, dear.'

'I don't think I've got any clean clothes, Gran.'

Gran frowned at me.

'Verity! What's the matter with you? There's at least ten different clean outfits hanging in your wardrobe. Now go and put something on *at once!*'

Gran doesn't often get cross, but when she uses that tone you can't argue with her.

I looked desperately at Grandad.

'Can't I stay in my fairy frock, Grandad?' I pleaded.

Grandad tutted at me. 'Do as Gran says, darling,' he said.

I looked at Dad.

'Upstairs, Verity. Quick sharp,' said Dad.

So I went upstairs, very very slowly. I stopped to listen halfway up.

'That's not like our Verity. She's usually such a good little girl, does as she's told and never any arguing.'

'Of course she's had a worrying time, lately.'

'Has she seemed upset at school, Miss Smith?'

'Well yes, she hasn't been her usual self at all. I agree, she's generally a lovely cheery little girl, a total joy to teach. But of course when she's had such a devastatingly terrible bereavement to deal with—'

'Bereavement?' said Dad. 'We don't know for sure that Mabel's dead.'

'We've done our best to advertise.'

'She might come back yet. It's a bit soon to give up hope – though she's never run away before.'

'But . . . I thought . . . Verity said . . . so her mum's left home?' said Miss Smith.

'Her *mum*?' said Gran. 'No no, my daughter passed away long ago.'

'When our little Verity was born,' said Grandad.

'Has Verity been talking about her mum at school, Miss Smith?' said Dad. 'I think she's been dreaming about her. It's been worrying me a lot. Perhaps you can help us. We've never been very good at talking about it—'

'It's too upsetting,' said Gran.

'Of course she didn't ever know her mum,' said Grandad.

'I see,' said Miss Smith, though it was clear she didn't. 'So . . . who is Mabel?'

'Oh! That's our cat,' said Dad.

I gave a moan. Gran came whipping outside into the hall.

'Verity! Are you hanging about on the stairs listening to us? I told you to go and get some sensible clean clothes on!'

'I can't, Gran!'

'Whatever's the matter with you today?' said Gran crossly. 'Why are you showing me up in front of Miss Smith? And what have you been *saying* to her?'

I hung my head, unable to explain. Gran sighed. She took hold of my arm and started pulling me up the stairs.

'No, Gran! Please! Don't!' I whimpered, realizing where we were heading.

Gran tugged me into the bedroom. She stopped to get her breath. She sniffed.

'What *is* that smell?'

'I . . . I'm not sure,' I said, which was the biggest lie yet, because I was surer than sure.

My eyes swivelled towards the wardrobe. So did Gran's. She stepped towards it.

'Don't!'

But she did. She flung the door open – and then reeled backwards, choking.

'Oh my goodness! What on *earth* . . . ?' She bent down and saw the duffle bag at the back.

'There's your duffle bag! Is that where the awful smell is coming from? Don't say you've left your wet swimming things in there all this time?'

She seized the duffle bag, pulled it out into the open, undid the top . . . and tipped the contents onto my carpet.

Then Gran screamed and screamed and screamed. Dad came running. Miss Smith came running. Grandad came hobbling.

Gran went on screaming for a long, long time. Even after she was downstairs and trembling in her armchair and Miss Smith had poured her a cup of strong sweet tea, Gran still made little gaspy sounds.

Dad and Grandad made loud gagging sounds as they shovelled poor Mabel and her duffle bag into a big black plastic rubbish sack and carted her outside into the garden. Then they washed and washed and washed.

I wept until the front of my stupid fairy frock was sodden.

Miss Smith made a fresh pot of tea when Dad and Grandad came back.

'I'm so sorry,' Gran gasped. 'I should have made the tea. Whatever must you think of us?'

'I reckon you got more than you bargained for when you brought our Verity's purse back!' said Grandad.

'Verity?' said Dad.

They all looked at me. I wept harder.

'Don't cry so, pet. I'm not cross. I'm just . . . puzzled. *Why* did you hide Mabel in your duffle bag? And why did you wrap her up like that?'

'It was bandages. Did you think it would make her better?' said Grandad.

'Bandages!' said Miss Smith.

She looked at me. I looked at her.

'Oh dear, oh dear!' said Miss Smith. 'You tried to make Mabel into a cat mummy!'

☆ CHAPTER EIGHT ☆

Mabel R.I.P.

It all came out. Gran was very upset, wondering how I could have done such a silly, shameful thing. Grandad started spluttering with laughter. Dad was fussed because I hadn't said anything the moment I'd found Mabel.

'I *couldn't*,' I shouted. 'She was dead. We don't talk about anyone being dead because we all get upset and dead people have to be buried and I couldn't bury Mabel because she's frightened of outdoors and she'd hate to be buried under the dirty earth with all the worms.'

I thought they'd all be cross with me for shouting like that. Not a bit of it! They looked shocked. Then they all

started being very *kind*. Gran sat me on her lap and Grandad said he'd donate his special toolbox as a coffin and Mabel would stay safe inside. Miss Smith said I could maybe paint the toolbox with Egyptian signs so that it would be like a special mummy case. She said the very first Ancient Egyptians used very similar wooden boxes. If I painted big Egyptian eyes on the side of the box then this would mean Mabel could look out, and I could also paint a special door so her spirit could get in and out of the coffin.

'A special little cat-flap door,' I said, blowing my nose. 'That's right, Verity,' said Miss Smith, giving me a hug. It was as if she'd stopped being my teacher and was now a member of my family.

Dad had a little private word with her. I couldn't hear much until right at the end. Miss Smith said I was her special favourite in her class. She really did! I wish I could tell Sophie and Laura and Aaron. I especially wish I could tell Moyra. But I know it's a secret. And I'd hate it if Miss Smith told *my* secret to the whole class.

After Miss Smith went Gran started a very, very long session with disinfectant and scrubbing brush in my wardrobe while all my clothes whirled round and round in the washing machine. Grandad took all his tools out of the toolbox and cleaned it up and sanded it down so it was smooth for me to paint on.

Dad helped me do the painting. It was getting quite late by this time but we all knew Mabel couldn't wait much longer to be buried. I needed to wear something more sombre than a fairy outfit and all my clothes were being washed, so I took another of Gran's old sheets and wrapped it round and round me and secured it with a purple chocolate ribbon. I looked almost like an Ancient Egyptian myself.

Dad and Grandad went into the garden with the box. They wouldn't let me come while they were putting Mabel into her new coffin. They wouldn't let me kiss her bye. So I went to the hearthrug in the living room where some of Mabel's cat hair still lingered. I curled up very small and kissed the soft spot on the rug where Mabel always put her head.

Then Dad and Grandad called me and I went outside. Mabel was safely entombed in the box. There was still rather a smell wafting around the garden but it couldn't be helped. Dad had already started digging a big hole down by the apple tree at the bottom of the garden. Grandad dug too. I got my old baby spade and dug as well, though I got the sheet a bit muddy. It was getting dark so I couldn't see if there were any worms. It was maybe just as well.

It took *ages* to make the hole big enough. Gran came out and said I should go to bed and Mabel could be buried in the morning now she was safe in her box, but Dad said it was important to have the ceremony now.

At last the hole gaped wide enough for Dad and Grandad to lower Mabel in her box down into it. Grandad let me pick a little bunch of his roses. I scattered the petals on top of Mabel.

'Perhaps you'd like to say something, Verity?' said Dad.

'Dear Mabel, I love you and I'm so sorry I shouted at you. Please be

happy in your after-life and fly back and see if you can visit me. You're the best cat in the world and I *wish* I could have preserved you as a proper mummy . . .' I started to cry and couldn't carry on.

'But you will always be preserved in our memory,' said Dad.

Then he trickled a handful of earth onto the petal-strewn box. Grandad did too. They looked at me.

'I wish we didn't have to cover her up,' I said.

'It's like planting a bulb,' said Grandad. 'Mabel will make lots of lovely flowers grow in the spring.'

I fidgeted. I didn't think Mabel was *remotely* like a bulb. I didn't want her to grow into flowers. I wanted her to grow back into herself so I could cuddle her and love her and keep her for ever.

'Couldn't we just keep her in her box now?' I said.

'*Not* a good idea,' said Grandad.

'We have to make sure she's safe and undisturbed,' said Dad. 'But I know just how you feel, Verity. When . . . when your mum died . . . the burying bit was the hardest of all.' He reached for my hand and held it tight. 'But we have to do it and there's no way of making it better. You're going to miss Mabel terribly. We all are. But gradually it stops hurting quite so badly.'

'Do you still hurt about Mum, Dad?' I whispered.

'A lot of the time, yes. And Gran does. And Grandad. But although I'm sad some of the time I'm also happy too. And you will be as well, I promise. Now let's say goodbye to Mabel.'

'Goodbye Mabel,' I said, and I took a handful of earth and carefully sprinkled it over her.

Then I went back inside while Dad and Grandad covered Mabel up.

Gran was putting another batch of my clothes in the washing machine.

'Honestly!' she said, shaking her head at me. But then she gave me a big hug and made me a mug of hot chocolate because I'd got cold staying out in the garden so long.

My bedroom smelt very strongly of disinfectant when I went up to bed. I looked sadly at the empty wardrobe. I wished I could have kept Mabel as a mummy. I wished she was still alive. I wished I hadn't been mean to her. I felt very sad . . . but I felt peaceful instead of worried.

I didn't tell Sophie or Laura or Aaron what I'd done when I went to school the next morning. I certainly didn't tell Moyra. Sophie asked straight away if Mabel had come back. I took a deep breath.

'Yes. I found her. But she was dead. So we buried her in the garden.'

Sophie put her arm round me. So did Laura. Aaron looked awkward and mumbled that he was very, very sorry. Moyra started asking questions, wondering where I'd found Mabel and what she looked like. She asked if she'd started to go mouldy.

'Shut up,' I said. 'I don't want to talk about it.'

Sophie and Laura and Aaron told Moyra to shut up too. So she did.

I was tremendously relieved that Miss Smith didn't breathe a word about Mabel at school. She didn't single me out in any way or act like I was her special favourite. She was so just-like-any-old-

teacher that I started to feel a bit disappointed, but when the bell went for going-home time she asked me to come and see her.

'I wonder why Miss Smith wants you, Verity?' said Sophie.

'I hope she's not cross with you,' said Laura.

'I hope she *is*,' said Moyra.

'I hope she doesn't keep you long. You've got to come up to the park today, you haven't been for *ages*,' said Aaron.

Miss Smith didn't keep me long. She just smiled at me and asked me gently how I was.

'I still feel really bad about Mabel,' I said.

'Of course you do,' said Miss Smith. 'Look, I've found you a book that tells you all about the Egyptian Book of the Dead. It's full of magic spells and prayers for dead people.'

'Is there one for dead cats?' I asked eagerly.

'I'm not sure. Perhaps you can make one up. You could write it out in your best handwriting and do a special picture of Mabel. Maybe you could make your own little book about her? You could stick in photos and write about all the happy times you had with her. It could be a special way of remembering her for always.'

'I like that idea!' I said. Then I added shyly, 'And I like you, Miss Smith. In fact you've always been *my* special favourite.'

Miss Smith laughed and went pink and told me to run along.

I went up to the park with Gran and Aaron and Aaron's mum and baby Aimee and Licky.

We passed some of the Mabel posters on the way. I hung my head and felt sad, but in the park Licky caught this little boy's ball and wouldn't give it back and we all had to play Chase the Dog and it was such fun that I almost forgot about Mabel.

I remembered her when we got home though. I went back into the garden and knelt by her grave and whispered to her. The earth was packed tight so it didn't look as if her spirit had flown out of the box yet.

Grandad called me to come in but I didn't want to. Grandad came out into the garden and kept me company for a bit. Then Dad got home and came and put his arm round me.

'You've been early three days in a row, Dad!' I said.

'I'm going to try to get away early *every* day now,' said Dad. 'I think we need to spend more time with each other, Verity. You know it's so stupid, I've spent such a long time feeling sad that your mummy died, and yet I should also be feeling so very glad that I've got you.'

He said it as if he'd been rehearsing what to say all the way home from work, but it still sounded good.

He asked if Miss Smith had said anything at school and I told him about doing a book about Mabel.

'That's a wonderful idea! Miss Smith is *so* clever. You're very lucky to have such a lovely teacher, Verity,' said Dad. 'It's Saturday tomorrow, so we'll go shopping for a special notebook for Mabel.'

☆ CHAPTER NINE ☆

The Egyptian Book of the Dead Mabel

We ended up buying two special big blank books. One for Mabel. And one for my mum.

'You can do Mabel's book all by yourself, Verity,' said Dad. 'And we'll work on Mummy's book together, just you and me. I want you to know all about her.'

'Don't you mind me talking about her now?'

'I don't mind a bit. I think we should talk. I was silly not to before.'

'Can I talk about her to Gran and Grandad too?'

'Maybe that's not such a good idea. Gran still finds it too sad.'

'Dad, did Miss Smith tell you to talk about my mum?' I asked.

Dad went a bit red.

'Well . . . we did sort of . . . yes, it was really her idea,' he said.

'She has great ideas, doesn't she?' I said. 'I do like her. Do you like her, Dad?'

'Mmm. Yes. I like her a lot,' said Dad, and he went even redder. He smiled. I smiled too.

We worked on our books all weekend.

A BOOK ABOUT MUMMY

This is a picture of Mummy when she was a little girl. She looks just like Verity. (though I wouldn't wear a frock like that!)

Mummy liked reading and dancing and swimming and drawing when she was a little girl. (So do I!)

She always wanted a pet but Gran wasn't too keen. Mummy had to wait till

she was grown up and married to Daddy.

Then they had Mabel. (The best cat in the world.)

Mummy and Daddy wanted to have children very much. This is a picture of Mummy looking very happy because she was expecting a baby. (Me!)

You will never guess what! I've got a kitten now!

Sophie and her mum and dad came round on Sunday and said I could choose one of their kittens. I wasn't sure at first. I badly wanted a kitten but it felt as if I was being unfair and disloyal to Mabel.

'I understand, Verity. But loving one cat a great deal doesn't mean you can never ever love another one,' said Dad. 'I should say "yes, please" to a kitten if I were you.'

So I went back to Sophie's house and we spent a long time playing with Sporty, Scary, Baby and Posh.

They were all so *sweet*. Sporty's already started to climb the curtains! Scary is very bold and chases after the clockwork frog. Posh is probably the prettiest and seems to know it, stretching out elegantly as if she's posing. But Baby is the cuddliest.

'You can have whichever one you like,' said Sophie. 'Only I rather hope you won't choose Sporty as she's such a pickle. And Scary's so funny. And Posh just looks so perfect.'

It was no problem at all choosing. I desperately wanted Baby.

So now I have my very own kitten and I love her to bits. I'm going to look after her properly and I shall never ever be cross with her. I hope she lives until long after I'm grown up. But I know one thing. I'll never love Baby *quite* as much as I loved my Mabel . . .

ODD ONE OUT

☆ ODD ONE OUT ☆

I'm the odd one out in the family. There are a lot of us. OK, here goes. There's my mum and my stepdad Graham and my big brother Mark and my big sister Ginnie and my little sister Jess and my big stepbrother Jon and my big stepsister Alice, and then there's my little half-sister Cherry and my baby half-brother Rupert. And me, Laura. Not to mention my real dad's new baby and his girlfriend Gina's twins, but they live in Cornwall now so I only see them for holidays. Long holidays, like summer and sometimes Christmas and Easter. Not short bank holidays, like today. It's a bank holiday and that means an Outing.

I hate Outings. I like Innings. My idea of bliss would be to read my book in bed with a packet of Pop Tarts for breakfast, get up late and draw or colour or write stories, have bacon sandwiches and crisps and a big cream cake or two for lunch, read all afternoon, have a whole chocolate Swiss roll for tea in front of the telly, draw or colour or write more stories, and then pizza for supper.

I've never enjoyed a day like that. It wouldn't work anyway because there are far too many of us if we all stay indoors, and the big ones hog the sofa and the comfy chairs, and the little ones are always dashing around and yelling and grabbing my felt tips. And Mum is always trying to stop me eating all the food I like best, pretending that a plate of lettuce and carrots and celery is just as yummy as pizza(!), and Graham is always suggesting I might like to get on this bike he bought me and go for a ride.

I wish he'd get on *his* bike. And take the whole family with him. And most of mine. Imagine if it was just Mum and me . . .

We had to do a piece of autobiographical writing at school last week on 'My Family'. I pondered for a bit. Just writing down the *names* of my family would take up half the page. I wanted to write a proper story, not an autobiographical list. So I had an imaginary cull of my entire family apart from Mum, and wrote about our life together as a teeny-weeny two-people family. I went into painstaking detail, writing about birthdays and Christmas and how my mum sometimes produced presents that had *Love from Daddy* or *Best Wishes from Auntie Kylie in Australia* – although I knew she'd really bought them herself. I even pretended that Mum sometimes played at being my gran or even grandpa and I played at being her son or her little baby. I wrote that although we played these games it was just for fun. We weren't lonely at all. We positively *loved* being such a small family.

Mrs Mann positively loved my effort too! This was a surprise because Mrs Mann is very, very strict. She's the oldest teacher at school and she can be really scary and sarcastic. You can't mess around in Mrs Mann's class. She wears these neat grey suits that match her grey hair, and white blouses with tidily tied bows, and a pearl brooch precisely centred on her lapel. You can tell just by looking at her that she's a stickler for punctuation and spelling and paragraphing and all those other boring, boring, boring things that stop you getting on with the story. My piece had its fair share of mistakes ringed in Mrs Mann's red rollerball, but she *still* gave me a ten out of ten because she said it was such a vivid, truthful piece of heartfelt writing.

I felt a little fidgety about this. Vivid it might be, but truthful it *isn't*. When Mrs Mann was talking about my small family, my friends Amy and Kate stared at me open-mouthed because I'm always whining on to them about my *big* family. Luckily they're not tell-tales.

Sometimes I get on better with all my Steps. My big stepbrother Jon likes art too, and he always says sweet things about my drawings. My big stepsister Alice isn't bad either. One day when we were all bored she did my hair in these cool little plaits with beads and ribbons, and made up my face so I looked almost grown up. Yes, I like Jon and Alice, but they're much older than me so they don't really want me hanging out with them.

The Halfies aren't bad either. I quite like sitting Cherry on my lap and reading her *Where the Wild Things Are*. She always squeals when I roar their terrible roars right in her ear and Mum gets cross, but

Cherry *likes* it. Rupert isn't into books yet – in fact I was a bit miffed when I showed him my old nursery-rhyme book and he *bit* it, like he thought it was a big bright sandwich. He's not really fun to play with yet because he's too little.

That's the trouble. Mark and Ginnie and Jon and Alice are too big. Jess and Cherry and Rupert are too little. I'm the Piggy in the Middle.

Hmm. My unpleasant brother Mark frequently makes grunting snorty noises at me and calls me Fatty Pigling.

I have highly inventive nicknames for Mark – indeed, for *all* my family (apart from Mum) – but I'd better not write them down or you'll be shocked.

I said a few very rude words to myself when Mum and Graham said we were going for a l-o-n-g walk along the river for our bank holiday outing. It's OK for Rupert. He goes in the buggy. It's OK for Cherry and Jess. They get piggyback rides the minute they start whining. It's OK for Mark and Ginnie and Jon and Alice. They stride ahead in a little gang (or lag behind, whatever), and they talk about music and football and s-e-x, and whenever I edge up to them they say, 'Push off, Pigling,' if they're Mark or Ginnie, or, 'Hi, Laura, off you go now,' if they're Jon or Alice.

I'd love it if it could just be Mum and me going on a walk together. But Graham is always around and he makes silly jokes or slaps me on the back or bosses me about. Sometimes I get really narked and tell him he's not my dad so he can't tell me what to do. Other times I just *look* at him. Looks can be very effective.

My face was contorted in a *dark scowl* all the long, long, long trudge along the river. It was so incredibly boring. I am past the age of going 'Duck duck duck' whenever a bird with wings flies past. I am not yet of the age to collapse into giggles when some male language students with shades say hello in sexy foreign accents (Ginnie and Alice), and I don't stare gape-mouthed when a pretty girl in a bikini waves from a boat (Mark and Jon).

I just stomped around wearily, surreptitiously eating a Galaxy . . . and then a Kit Kat . . . and a couple of Rolos. I handed the rest round to the family like a good generous girl. That's another huge disadvantage of large families. Offer your packet of Rolos round once and they're nearly all gone in one fell swoop.

We went to this pub garden for lunch and I golloped down a couple of cheese toasties and two packets of crisps and two Cokes – all this fresh air had made me peckish – and I had to stoke myself up for the long trail back home along the river.

'Oh, we thought we'd go via the Green Fields,' said Graham.

I groaned. 'Graham! It's *miles*! And I've got serious blisters already.'

'I think you might like the Green Fields this particular Monday,' said Mum.

She and Graham smiled.

I didn't smile back. I *don't* like the Green Fields. They are just what their name implies. Two big green fields joined by a line of poplar trees. They don't even have a playground with swings. There isn't even an ice-cream van. There's just a lot of *grass*.

But guess what, guess what! When we got nearer the Green Fields I heard this buzz and clatter and music and laughter.

And *then* I smelled wonderful mouth-watering fried onions. We turned the corner – and the Green Fields were so full you couldn't see a glimpse of grass! There was a fair there for the bank holiday.

I gave a whoop. Mark and Ginnie and Jon and Alice gave a whoop too, though they were half mocking me. Jess and Cherry gave great big whoops. Baby Rupert whooped too. He couldn't see the fair down at kneecap level in his buggy but he didn't want to be left out.

Mum and Graham smiled smugly.

Of course, the fair meant different things to all of us. Jon and Mark – *and* Graham – wanted to go straight on the dodgems. Ginnie and Alice and I went too, while Mum minded the littlies. She bought them all whippy ice creams with chocolate flakes. I wailed, saying I'd much much much sooner have an ice cream than get in a dodgem car. Mum sighed and bought me an ice cream too. But as soon as it was in my hand I decided it *might* be fun to go on the dodgems too, so I jumped in beside Jon.

Big mistake. Mark drove straight into us, *wham-bam*, and then *splat*, the chocolate flake went right up my nostril and my ice cream went all over my face.

Mum mopped me up with one of Rupert's wet wipes, and Jon bought me another ice cream to console me. I licked this in peace while Jess and Cherry and baby Rupert sat in a kiddies' roundabout and slowly and solemnly revolved in giant teacups.

'I wonder if they've got a *proper* roundabout,' said Mum. 'I used to love those ones with the horses and the twisty gilt rails and the special music. I want to go on a real old-fashioned carousel.'

'Oh, Mum, you don't get those any more,' said Ginnie – but she was *wrong*.

We went on all sorts of *new*-fashioned rides first. We were all hurtled round and round and upside down until even I started wondering if that extra ice cream had been a good idea. Then, as we staggered queasily to the other side of the field, we heard old organ music. Mum lifted her head, listening intently.

'Is it?' she said.

It *was*. We pushed through the crowd and suddenly it was just like stepping back a hundred years. There was the most beautiful old roundabout with galloping horses with grinning mouths and flaring nostrils and scarlet saddles, some shiny black, some chocolate brown, some dappled grey. There was also one odd pink ostrich with crimson feathers and an orange beak.

'Why is that big bird there, Mum?' I asked.

'I don't know, Laura. I think they always have one odd one. Maybe it's a tradition.'

'I'm going to go on the bird,' I said.

The roundabout was slowing down. Mum had little Rupert unbuckled from his buggy so he could ride too. Graham had Cherry in his arms. Mark and Jon said the roundabout was just for kids, but when Graham asked one of them to look after Jess they both offered eagerly. Ginnie and Alice had an argument over who was going to ride on a black horse with ROBBIE on his nameplate (they both have a thing about Robbie Williams) so eventually they squeezed on together.

I rushed for the ostrich. I didn't need to. No one else wanted it. Well, *I* did. I clambered on and stroked its crimson feathers. Ostriches are definitely the odd ones out of the bird family. They can't fly. They're too heavy for their own wings.

I'm definitely the odd one out of my family – and I frequently feel too heavy for my own legs. I sat gripping the ostrich with my knees, waiting for the music to start and the roundabout to start revolving. People were still scrabbling onto the few remaining horses. A middle-aged lady in much-too-tight jeans was hauling this little toddler up onto the platform. I put out my hand to help – and then stopped, astonished. I couldn't have been more amazed if my ostrich had opened its beak and bitten me. It wasn't any old middle-aged lady bursting out of her jeans. It was Mrs Mann!

I stared at her – and she stared at me.

'Hello, Laura,' she said. 'This is my little granddaughter, Rosie.'

I made appropriate remarks to Rosie while Mrs Mann struggled to get them both up onto the ordinary brown horse beside my splendid ostrich. Mrs Mann couldn't help showing rather a lot of her vast blue-denimed bottom. I had to struggle to keep a straight face.

'Are you with your mother, Laura?' said Mrs Mann.

Oh help! Mum was in front of me with Rupert. I had written Mrs Mann that long essay about Mum and me just living together. I hadn't mentioned any babies whatsoever.

'I'm here . . . on my own,' I mumbled.

At that exact moment Mum turned round and waved at me. 'Are you all right, Laura?' she called. She nodded at Mrs Mann.

Mum and Mrs Mann looked at me, waiting for me to introduce

them. I stayed silent as the music started up. *Go, go, go*, I urged inside my head. But we didn't go soon enough.

'I'm Laura's mum,' said Mum.

'I'm Laura's teacher,' said Mrs Mann. 'And this is Rosie.'

Rosie waved coyly to Rupert.

'This is my baby Rupert,' said Mum.

Mrs Mann looked surprised.

'And that's Cherry over there with my partner Graham, and Jess with my son Mark, and that's my stepson Jon, and then that's Alice and Ginnie over there, waving at those boys, the naughty girls. Sorry! We're such a big family now that it's a bit hard for anyone to take in,' said Mum, because Mrs Mann was looking so stunned.

The horses started to edge forward very very slowly, u-u-u-u-p and d-o-w-n. My tummy went up and down too as Mrs Mann looked at me.

'So you're part of a very big family, Laura?' she said.

'Yes, Mrs Mann,' I said, in a very small voice.

'Well, you do surprise me,' she said.

'Nana, Nana!' said Rosie, taking hold of Mrs Mann's nose and wiggling it backward and forward affectionately. Mrs Mann simply chuckled. I wondered how she'd react if any of our class tweaked her nose!

'We seem to be surprising each other,' shouted Mrs Mann, as the music got louder as the roundabout revved up. 'Well, Laura, judging by your long and utterly convincing autobiographical essay, you are obviously either a pathological liar – or a born writer. We'll give you the benefit of the doubt. You have the most vivid imagination of any child I've ever taught. You will obviously go far.'

And then the music was too loud for talking and the horses whirled round and round and round. I sat tight on my ostrich, and it spread its crimson wings and we flew far over the fair, all the way up and over the moon.

LIZZIE
ZIPMOUTH

To Naomi
With many thanks

☆ CHAPTER ONE ☆

Do you ever have nightmares? I had such a scary dream I didn't want to go back to sleep. It was just starting to get light. I sat up in bed and looked at Mum. Her hair was spread out over the pillow.

I wish I had lovely long hair like Mum. Sometimes she lets me brush and comb it. I can do it in a funny topknot. Once I put it in plaits and Mum looked just like my sister, not my mum.

  I haven't got a real sister. Or a real brother. But today I was getting two new sort-of brothers, Rory and Jake.

I didn't like them much.

I was getting a stepdad too. He was called Sam. I didn't call him anything. I didn't like him at *all*.

I frowned at my mum. I took hold of a little clump of her hair and pulled.

'Ouch! What are you up to, Lizzie?' said Mum, opening one eye.

'I was just waking you up,' I said.

'It's too early to wake up,' said Mum, putting her arm round me. 'Let's snuggle down and have a snooze.'

'I don't want to snuggle,' I said, wriggling away. 'Mum, *why* do we have to move in with Sam?'

Mum sighed. 'Because I love him.'

'*I* don't love him,' I said.

'You might one day,' said Mum.

'Never ever,' I said.

'You wait and see,' said Mum. 'I think you're going to love being part of a big family. You and me and Sam and Rory and Jake.'

'I don't want to be a big family,' I said. 'I want to be a little family. Just you and me in our own flat.'

We had fun together, Mum and me.

We went to football matches and we shared big tubs of ice-cream and we danced to music.

Sometimes I stayed up really late and then we went to bed together. I didn't like night-time because of the bad dreams.

I dreamt about my first stepdad.

I hate stepdads. I've got a real dad but I don't see him now. He stopped living with us ages ago. He doesn't come to see me but I don't care any more.

My first stepdad doesn't come to see us either and I'm very, very glad about that. He was a scary monster stepdad. He pretended to be jolly and friendly at first. He bought me heaps of presents. He even bought me a Flying Barbie. I always badly wanted a Barbie doll but Mum never bought me one. She thinks they're too girly. I *like* girly things. I loved my Flying Barbie but I didn't ever love my first stepdad, even at the beginning.

When we went to live with him he was still jolly and friendly when he was in a good mood but he started to get lots of bad moods. He started shouting at me. I tried shouting back and he smacked me. He said I got on his nerves. He certainly got on *my* nerves. He said he didn't like me. I didn't like him one bit.

Mum didn't like him any more either, especially when he shouted at me. We left that stepdad. We went back to being just Mum and me.

We got our own flat. It was very small and poky and the bathroom had black mould and the heating didn't work, but it didn't matter. We were safe again, Mum and me.

But then Mum met this man, Sam, in a sandwich bar. They ate lots and lots of sandwiches. Then they started going out together. Then *I* had to start going out with them at weekends even though I didn't want to. Sam's sons, Rory and Jake, came too. They didn't see their mum any more. They seemed to like my mum. But I didn't like their dad.

'I don't want Sam to be my stepdad,' I said. Again.

'He's not a bit like the last one, Lizzie, I promise,' said Mum.

I love my mum but I don't always believe her, even when she promises.

'Lizzie?' said Mum. 'Oh come on, don't look like that. Don't we have fun together when we all go out, the five of us?'

Mum had fun. She larked about with Sam and sang silly songs and talked all the time and held his hand.

Sam had fun. He laughed at my mum and sang with her and told her these stupid jokes and put his arm round her.

Rory had fun. He played football with Mum and she taught him how to dive when we went swimming and when he couldn't choose between pizza and pasta at the restaurant he was allowed to have both.

Jake had fun. He ate sweets all day long and Mum gave him a musical toothbrush so that all the sugar wouldn't rot his teeth too much. He brushed his teeth all day long too. He had thirteen Beanie Babies that he carried round with him. They all had to have their teeth brushed too.

I didn't have fun. I thought Jake was a silly baby. And it wasn't fair. Mum didn't mind him having his Beanie Babies. Boys are allowed to be girly.

I didn't like Rory much either. He pushed me over when we played football. I don't think he meant to but it still hurt. And he splashed me when we went swimming. He *did* mean to do that.

I *certainly* didn't like Sam. I knew he wouldn't be jolly and friendly for long. I was waiting for the shouting to start.

He kept trying to make friends with me. I just looked down at the floor and wouldn't say a word.

I decided not to say a word to anyone.

☆ CHAPTER TWO ☆

I didn't say a word when I had my breakfast. I didn't say a word when I got washed and dressed. I didn't say a word when I packed up my books and my crayons and my stickers and my schoolbag and my washing things and my hairbrush and all my underwear and my T-shirts and shorts and trousers and jumpers and my duffel coat and my welly boots. I didn't even say a word when Mum threw my old cosy dressing-gown and last year's party dress and my school uniform in the rubbish bin.

Mum said my dressing-gown was all stained and my party dress was so small it showed my knickers and I'd be going to a new school after the summer holidays with a different uniform.

I felt stained and small and different in the car with Sam and Rory and Jake. They came to fetch us and help us with all our luggage.

'It's going to be lovely living in a house instead of that crummy little flat,' said Mum. 'Won't it be great to have a garden, Lizzie? You can play football with Rory.'

'Well, I usually play football with the boys next door,' said Rory. 'But I suppose Lizzie can join in if she wants.'

I didn't want. But I didn't say anything.

'You'll like the swing, Lizzie,' said Mum. 'Imagine having your own swing!'

'It's *my* swing,' said Jake.

'But you won't mind sharing it with Lizzie, will you?' said Sam.

Jake looked as if he minded a lot. I didn't want to go on his silly old swing anyway. But I didn't say anything.

'I don't have to share my bedroom with Lizzie, do I?' Jake asked suspiciously. 'Because there's not room. Not with all my Beanie Babies and their special beds.'

They weren't real beds. Jake had thirteen shoe boxes with paper tissues for bedcovers. Mum acted like she thought this was sweet. *I* thought it was stupid. But I didn't say anything.

'I've got all my football souvenirs and my rock collection and my

worm garden in my bedroom,' Rory said quickly. 'I wouldn't mind sharing my bedroom with Lizzie but I have to warn her that the worms wriggle around a lot. They *could* just end up in her bed.'

I decided I'd mind that very much indeed. But I didn't say anything.

I stood close to Mum. She knew I wanted to share *her* bedroom. But she had Sam now.

'Lizzie can have her very own special bedroom,' said Sam. 'We can turn my study into Lizzie's room. My computer can easily fit into our bedroom.'

'There! Aren't you lucky, Lizzie?' said Mum.

I didn't feel at all lucky.

'I wonder what sort of bedroom you'd like, Lizzie? You can choose the colour for the walls and we'll get you curtains and a duvet to match,' said Sam. 'What about . . . pink?'

'Pink's a bit girly,' said Mum. 'How about red, Lizzie? Or purple?'

I liked pink. But I didn't say anything.

Sam painted the walls purple and Mum bought red-and-purple checked curtains and a matching duvet. Sam bought a real little red armchair and a purple fluffy rug.

'There! Isn't it lovely? What do you say, Lizzie?' said Mum.

I didn't say anything.

'*Why* don't you ever say anything, Lizzie?' said Rory. 'It's like you've got a zip across your mouth.'

'Lizzie Zipmouth,' said Jake, giggling. 'Can't you talk at all?'

'Don't call Lizzie silly names,' said Sam. 'Of course she can talk. She's just feeling a bit shy at the moment.' He looked round my new bedroom. 'How can we make it a bit more homely for Lizzie? What about your toys? Shall we spread them around a bit?'

I didn't have that many. They all fitted neatly in
a drawer. I wished I still had Flying Barbie but she
got left behind when we ran away from that first
stepdad. I hope she managed to fly out the window
away from him.

I wished it was time to leave this second stepdad.
He was being jolly and friendly but he'd change soon.
I was still waiting for the shouting to start. I was sure he was just
pretending to be kind.

I wasn't so sure about Rory. Maybe he really *was* kind. He stuck
one of his Manchester United posters up on my bedroom wall.

'There! It's the right colour,' he said.

Sam wanted Jake to give me one of his Beanie Babies. Jake didn't
want to be kind.

'They're *mine*,' he said. 'I don't want to give them to Lizzie Zipmouth.'

'Hey, stop the name-calling,' said Sam. 'What about the little purple teddy? He'd like to live in Lizzie's room.'

'No, he wouldn't!' said Jake. 'He'd *hate* it!'

I hated it in my room too. All that bright red and purple hurt my eyes. I opened up my new wardrobe and shut myself inside.

It was lonely in the wardrobe. I put my slippers on my hands and made them do a dance in the dark but I couldn't think of any other games I could play.

After a while I heard Rory calling for me. And then Mum and Sam and even Jake.

'Lizzie?'

'Lizzie, where *are* you?'

'Lizzie Zipmouth?'

They shouted and shouted and shouted and shouted.

I still didn't say anything at all. I kept my mouth well and truly zipped.

☆ CHAPTER THREE ☆

I got into big trouble with Mum when she found me. She was very, very cross because she thought I'd run away. She shouted at me.

Sam didn't shout at me. I was surprised. But maybe he *wanted* me to run away?

'You made your mum cry,' said Rory.

'You're ever so naughty, Lizzie Zipmouth,' said Jake.

Mum wanted me to say sorry to everyone for hiding in the wardrobe. I wouldn't say anything. So I got sent to bed without any tea.

I decided I didn't care one bit. But then Sam knocked on the door and whispered my name. He came into my room. I hid under the duvet. I was sure he was going to shout now.

But he didn't say anything at all. Long after he'd gone I peeped out. He'd left a big chocolate bar beside my bed. Purple to match my bedroom.

Rory and Jake crept in when they came to bed at the normal time. Rory gave me a biscuit. It was a bit crumbly from being in his pocket. I didn't say anything but I did smile at him. Jake didn't bring me any food but he ran and fetched his purple Beanie Baby teddy. 'You can have Mr Purple just for one night,' he said. 'Only you will give him back in the morning, won't you, Lizzie Zipmouth?'

I didn't say anything but I nodded at him.

I didn't touch the chocolate but I nibbled an edge of biscuit and cuddled Mr Purple. Then I snuggled down to go to sleep.

Then guess what? Mum came in with a tray of tea for me. I didn't have to say sorry. In fact Mum said sorry to me! She gave me a big, big cuddle and she cried. She promised she'd never ever get cross again. But as I said, I don't always believe Mum's promises.

The next day was Sunday. Mum and I used to have lovely fun Sundays when we were just a family of two. We'd lie in bed late and play Bears-in-Caves under the bedcovers and once Mum let me take a jar of honey to bed with us and she just laughed when the sheets got all sticky.

Mum liked reading the newspapers all morning. I liked drawing on the papers, giving all the ladies in the photos moustaches and the men long

dangly earrings. Then we'd have a picnic lunch in the park. We even had picnics when it was raining. We didn't care. We just said it was lovely weather for ducks and went, 'Quack quack quack.' Then we watched videos in the evening. Mum liked old black-and-white movies and I liked new brightly coloured cartoons.

We had LOVELY Sundays.

I didn't think I was going to like the new Sundays one bit. Mum and Sam had a lie-in. Rory and Jake had pillow fights and played on their computer. I sat in the wardrobe. I wished I had Mr Purple to keep me company but he was back in his box in Jake's bedroom.

We all went out to the pub for Sunday lunch. I don't like proper meals like meat and vegetables and puddings. I cut mine into teeny-tiny pieces and didn't eat any of them.

Jake started messing about with his meal too. Sam told him off.

'It's not fair! Lizzie Zipmouth isn't eating hers properly.'

'I've told you and told you not to call Lizzie silly names,' said Sam. 'Eat up at once, Jake!'

'And you eat up too, Lizzie,' said Mum.

I zipped my lips shut tight.

'She's a silly baby,' said Jake, dropping his forkful of potato onto his plate so that gravy splashed all over Mum.

'You're both silly babies,' said Mum. 'Oh dear, look at my white shirt! And I wanted to look extra smart to meet your grandma, Sam.'

We were going to have tea with this old, old lady. If she was Sam's grandma she was Rory and Jake's great-gran.

'So does that mean she's Lizzie's sort-of step-great-gran?' said Rory.

I've never had my own great-gran. I've got a granny at the seaside and a gran and grandpa in Scotland but I don't see any of them very often. I didn't want to see this sort-of step-great-gran either.

'My mum and dad live in Australia,' said Sam. 'So Great-Gran is very special for me.'

He said it as if special meant *scary*! 'She's OK, I suppose. But she's very strict,' said Rory. 'She tells me off if I talk in a slang sort of way. She says it sounds sloppy.'

'She says I *look* sloppy,' said Jake. 'She's always licking her hankie and wiping my face. Yuck! I *hate* that.'

I didn't want this old lady telling me off and wiping me. I looked at Mum. Mum looked as if she was worried about being told off and wiped too.

Great-Gran lived in a big block of flats. I hoped she might live right up at the top but she lived on the ground floor. Sam said it was to save her legs. I wondered if they were wearing out. Perhaps they were about to snap off at the socket like an old doll.

Great-Gran looked a bit like an old doll. This strange stiff little lady came to the door. She had very black hair combed so tightly into place it made her eyes pop. She creaked when she bent to hug Rory and Jake. She didn't hug me. She just looked me up and down. She looked Mum up and down too.

'It's lovely to meet you,' said Mum.

Great-Gran didn't look as if she thought it was lovely at all.

'Say hello to Rory and Jake's great-gran, Lizzie,' said Mum, though she knew I wouldn't.

And I didn't. I stared at the doormat. It said WELCOME. The doormat was telling fibs.

Great-Gran tutted. 'Well, you'd better come in,' she said.

Mum held my hand tight and we stepped inside.

'Dear, dear! Wipe your feet! Watch my beige carpet,' Great-Gran fussed.

But I wasn't watching her carpet. I was staring all round the walls in a daze. Hundreds of shining eyes were staring back at me!

☆ CHAPTER FOUR ☆

Dolls! Old china dolls in cream frocks and pinafores and little button boots, soft plush dolls with rosy cheeks and curls, baby dolls in long white christening robes, lady dolls with tiny umbrellas and high heels, a Japanese doll in a kimono with a weeny fan, dolls in school uniform and swimming costumes and party frocks, great dolls as big as me sitting in real wicker chairs, middle-sized dolls in row

after row on shelves, and tiny dolls no bigger than my thumb standing in their own green painted garden beside a doll's house.

'Great-Gran collects dolls,' said Rory unnecessarily.

'She doesn't collect Beanie Babies,' said Jake. 'Not even the rare ones.'

Sam patted my shoulder. 'Are you cold, Lizzie? You're shivering!' he said.

'Lizzie likes dolls,' said Mum.

'Well, I'm sure Gran won't mind her having a look at them,' said Sam – though he didn't sound sure at all.

'She can look, but she mustn't touch,' said Great-Gran.

I put my hands behind my back to show her I wouldn't touch even one tiny china hand.

'These are collector's dolls,' said Great-Gran. 'They're not for children.'

I nodded. I was very impressed. I thought I was too old for dolls but Great-Gran was very old indeed and she had hundreds. I knew exactly what I was going to be when I grew up. A doll collector!

I wandered very slowly and carefully round Great-Gran's flat. There were dolls on shelves all the way round her living room. She even had three special ballet dancer dolls on tippy-toes on top of her television set. She had a row of funny dolls with fat tummies on her kitchen window sill and a mermaid doll with a long shiny green tail in the bathroom. The dolls in her bedroom were all wearing their night-clothes, white nighties with pink ribbon trimming and blue-and-white striped pyjamas and soft red dressing-gowns with cords and tassels and little slippers with tiny pom-poms.

'Well? What do you think of them?' said Great-Gran, walking along briskly behind me.

I didn't say anything. But I must have had the right look on my face because Great-Gran gave me a little nod.

'I'd better go and put the kettle on,' she said. 'They won't have thought to do it, the gormless lot.'

I gave the littlest doll one last lingering glance. Her plaits were tied with tiny pink ribbons and she was holding a little pink rabbit no bigger than a button.

'I suppose you can stay in here looking,' she said. 'But only if you promise you won't touch.'

I did my pantomime of hands behind my back. But this wasn't good enough.

'*Promise* me,' said Great-Gran.

I didn't say anything but I tried so hard to make my face look as if I was promising that my eyes watered.

Great-Gran's eyes were a very bright blue even though she was such an old lady. They grew even brighter now.

'I can't hear you,' she said. She cupped her little claw hand behind her ear. 'Speak up!'

We looked at each other. I knew what she was up to. And she knew that I knew. We looked and looked and looked at each other.

'So you're not going to promise?' said Great-Gran.

'Come on then, out of the bedroom this instant.'

I looked at her pleadingly.

'What's the matter?' said Great-Gran. '*Why* can't you promise?'

I shook my head helplessly.

'Can't you talk?' said Great-Gran.

I shook my head.

'Of course you can talk if you really want to!' said Great-Gran. 'Open your mouth!'

She said it so fiercely I opened my mouth automatically.

'Aha!' said Great- Gran. 'There! You've got a tongue in your head after all. And two rows of shiny teeth. So use them, please, Madam. *Now!*'

My tongue and my teeth started working all by themselves. 'I promise!' I whispered. Great-Gran smiled triumphantly. All the dolls in her bedroom seemed to be smiling too.

Mum called out to me from the other room. I zipped my mouth shut again.

'Don't worry,' said Great-Gran. 'I won't tell the others.'

She put her finger to her lips. I put my finger to my lips.

'You're a caution, you are,' said Great-Gran. 'I'm pleased you like my dolls. You can come and visit me again. I have some more dolls stored in trunks. I *might* let you play with those dolls if you're a very, very good girl.'

☆ CHAPTER FIVE ☆

I was sometimes a very, very *bad* girl at Mum and Sam's place. I'd been a good girl with my first stepdad. They weren't going to catch me out again. Sam couldn't fool me. He'd turn out to be mean and scary like my first stepdad. Maybe he'd even be *worse*.

So, if Sam did the cooking I wouldn't eat any of it, even if it was one of my favourites, like pizza. If Sam chose a video I turned my chair round and wouldn't watch it, even when it was *Little Women* or *Black Beauty* or *The Secret Garden*. If Sam bought us ice-creams when we were out I wouldn't eat mine – not even when it was one of those big whippy ice-creams with strawberry sauce and a chocolate flake.

My mouth watered but I didn't even have one lick. The ice-cream melted and dripped down inside my sleeve.

'Honestly, Lizzie, why do you have to be so silly?' said Mum, sighing as she threw my ice-cream into the gutter.

Sam sighed too. I was *sure* he was going to shout at me this time. But he didn't.

He asked me if I'd like to go over and see Great-Gran again.

'Oh, Dad! Do we have to?' said Rory. 'I thought we only saw Great-Gran on Sundays.'

'We can't play properly at Great-Gran's. There's nothing to do,' said Jake.

'This is a special invitation for Lizzie,' said Sam. 'Shall I drive you over there after tea?'

I didn't know what to do. I wanted to go and see Great-Gran and her dolls very, very much. But I didn't want Sam to take me. I looked at Mum.

'I can't drive Sam's car, Lizzie,' she said.

I still looked at her.

'I can't come too. I have to stay here to keep an eye on Rory and Jake,' said Mum.

I looked at Mum. I looked at Sam.

'Coming, Lizzie?' said Sam.

I didn't say anything. I just gave a little nod.

Sam had to strap me into the seatbelt in the back of the car.

'Comfy?' he said.

I gave another teeny jerk of the head.

Sam played music as we drove, silly old children's songs about pink toothbrushes and mice with clogs and circus elephants. Sam sang them all.

'Feel free to join in,' he said.

I didn't sing. But my dangling feet did a little secret dance as Sam sang a song about a tiny house in a place with a very, very long funny name.

Sam took me into Great-Gran's flat but he didn't stay. He said he'd come back for me in an hour.

'She'll probably be bored in ten minutes,' said Great-Gran.

I wasn't the slightest bit bored. I had the most wonderful time ever. Great-Gran let me go on another tour round her flat. I looked at the dolls on shelves, the dolls on chairs, the dolls on the window sills, the dolls in their night-clothes ready for bed. Then I looked hopefully at Great-Gran. She looked back at me.

'What?' she said. Her eyes were gleaming as brightly as the dolls. I swallowed. My voice sounded rusty when I used it.

'Could I see the dolls in the trunk?' I whispered.

'Speak up!' said Great-Gran. 'And remember to say please!'

'Please could I see the dolls in the trunk. *Please*,' I said, so loudly that I nearly set the dolls on the shelves blinking.

'Certainly,' said Great-Gran. 'That's a very good girl! Come along then. You can help me get them out.'

She kept the trunks in the back of her built-in wardrobe. There were two, one on top of the other. I had to stand on tiptoe to reach the top one. 'Easy does it,' said Great-Gran.

I went so e-a-s-y I felt I was in slow motion. The trunk was heavy. There seemed to be several dolls inside. When Great-Gran lifted the lid I saw them lying in a row, eyes shut. They looked as if they were fast asleep.

'You can wake them up,' said Great-Gran.

I gently lifted a beautiful big doll with long blonde hair out of the trunk.

She had a white nightie but no slippers on her pale china feet. Her tiny toenails were painted pink. One of her hands was missing but I didn't mind a bit.

'She's beautiful!' I whispered, cradling her carefully.

'That's Alice. I expect she's a little chilly in that thin nightgown. Perhaps you'd like to find some clothes for her?' said Great-Gran.

The second trunk was crammed with neatly folded outfits – party frocks, winter coats trimmed with fur, sailor suits, checked pinafores, lace-edged underwear, black knitted stockings and little boots with tiny pearl buttons.

My hand hovered hopefully above the clothes.

'Go on, have a little sort through. But don't get them rumpled,' said Great-Gran.

I sifted through the clothes with trembling fingers and found a pale blue smocked dress with a white lace collar and a darker blue satin sash.

'Can she wear this one?'

'I think that's actually Alice's favourite outfit,' said Great-Gran.

I dressed Alice, moving her arms and legs very gently indeed. The blue sleeves were a little long for her, so her missing hand didn't show. She looked perfect.

Then I woke Sophie and Charlotte and little Edward and weeny Clementine and got them all dressed up. 'There! Don't they look smart? All ready for a party,' said Great-Gran, and she opened another box. There was a little blue-and-white doll's tea set inside.

I thought we'd pretend the party fare but Great-

Gran made real pink rosehip tea and opened a packet of tiny round iced biscuits that just fitted the plate.

We were still enjoying our party when Sam came to fetch me home. 'Have you enjoyed yourself, Lizzie?' he asked.

I didn't say anything. Not to Sam. But I nodded so hard my head hurt. When I kissed Great-Gran goodbye on her powdery cheek I whispered, 'Please can I come again?'

☆ CHAPTER SIX ☆

I went to see Great-Gran almost every day. I always played with Alice and Sophie and Charlotte and Edward and Clementine. Sometimes we had dolls' tea parties. Sometimes Great-Gran and I

had proper ladies' tea parties with big flowery cups and saucers and sandwiches and fairy cakes with pink icing and cherries. Great-Gran let me cut up my sandwich and cake to share with Alice and Sophie and Charlotte and Edward and Clementine.

Once Rory and Jake came too. Rory was polite to Great-Gran but he kept yawning and when he got home he ran all round the garden like crazy, leaping and whooping.

'It's great to be back! It's so b-o-r-i-n-g at Great-Gran's!' he yelled.

Sam said he could stick to Sunday visits.

'What about you, Jake?' said Sam.

'I don't know,' said Jake. 'I don't like the dolls much. But I quite like the tea party. I might want to take all my Beanie Babies.'

I frowned. Jake didn't play with his Beanie Babies *properly*. He got all silly and excited and threw them in the air and made them have fights. I was sure they'd knock the teacups over. Great-Gran would put Alice and Sophie and Charlotte and Edward and Clementine back in their trunk sharpish.

Sam put his arm round Mum.

'I take it you're not into dolls and tea parties either?'

'No way! Though I'm ever so glad Lizzie gets on so well with your gran. I'm a bit scared of her!' said Mum, giggling.

'Don't worry, she terrifies me!' said Sam.

'She can be seriously scary,' said Rory.

'She's so frowny,' said Jake.

'Well, I like her,' I said.

They all looked at me.

'Lizzie spoke!' said Rory.

'Lizzie unzipped!' said Jake.

Mum and Sam were smiling all over their faces. I smiled back. Then I skipped into my bright bedroom to get my knitting. I was making a teeny blue scarf for Alice. Great-Gran had taught me how to knit. She taught Jake too. Jake said he was going to make thirteen rainbow-striped scarves, one for each of his Beanie Babies, but he'd only done five rows of the first scarf so far. I'd nearly finished mine, but I seemed to have dropped several stitches somewhere. I needed to see Great-Gran to ask her to fix it.

We were going to see her on Sunday, the whole family. But on Friday night there was a phone call. It woke me up. I heard Sam on the phone. He sounded very worried. When I peeped out of my bedroom I saw his face was crumpled up the way Jake looks when he's about to cry.

'Oh dear, Lizzie, something very sad has happened,' said Sam, coming up the stairs. He put his arm round me. 'It's poor Great-Gran.'

'Is she dead?' I said, shivering.

'No, she's not dead, pet, but she's very ill. She's had a stroke. She can't walk or talk properly. She's in hospital. I'm going to see her now.'

'I'm coming too!'

'No, love, not now. It's much too late. Look, you're shivering. You hop into bed with Mum while I go to the hospital.'

Mum cuddled me close and told me to try to go back to sleep, but I couldn't. I kept thinking of Great-Gran lying on her back in a hospital bed unable to walk or talk, just like one of the dolls in the trunk.

☆ CHAPTER SEVEN ☆

Sam stayed at the hospital most of Saturday. Mum took Rory and Jake and me to football. It was a great game and our team scored. Rory and Jake jumped up and down and yelled and then remembered and drooped back in their seats, looking guilty.

'It's OK, boys,' said Mum, putting her arms round them. 'We can be sad about poor Great-Gran and happy about football too. Great-Gran wouldn't want you to stop enjoying the match.'

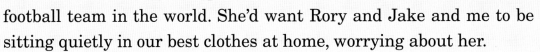

I looked at Mum. I knew Great-Gran much better than she did. Great-Gran thought football a waste of space. Great-Gran thought she was much more important than any football team in the world. She'd want Rory and Jake and me to be sitting quietly in our best clothes at home, worrying about her.

I *was* worrying.

'I want to see Great-Gran,' I said.

'I'm not sure they let young children into the hospital,' said Mum.

Rory and Jake breathed sighs of relief.

I cornered Sam when he came home that evening. He looked very tired and his eyes were red as if he might have been crying.

'I'll make you a cup of tea, Sam,' I said.

Sam looked very surprised.

'It's OK. I can make lovely tea. Great-Gran showed me how. And I hold the kettle ever so carefully so I can't scald myself.'

'You're a very clever girl, Lizzie,' said Sam. 'OK, then, I'd love a cup of tea.'

I made it carefully all by myself. Mum hovered but I wouldn't let her help. I carried the cup of tea in to Sam without spilling a drop.

'This is delicious tea,' said Sam, sipping. 'Thank you very much, Lizzie.'

'How is Great-Gran?' I asked.

'Not very well,' said Sam sadly.

'Is she going to get better?'

'I hope so.'

'Can she walk and talk yet?'

'She's going to have to learn all over again, like a baby. They're trying to teach her already. But she won't do as she's told.'

I nodded. I couldn't imagine Great-Gran letting anyone tell her what to do.

'Can I see her, Sam? Tomorrow?'

'I . . . I think you might find it a bit upsetting, pet,' said Sam.

'I know I'd find it upsetting,' said Rory.

'Please can I see her, Sam?' I begged.

'Lizzie, it's probably not a good idea,' said Mum.

'*Please*, Sam,' I said, clutch- ing his sleeve.

'OK then, Lizzie, if it's what you really want,' said Sam.

I hugged him – and sent his cup of tea flying. It went all over his trousers but he *still* didn't shout. He hugged me back!

Sam took me to the

hospital to see Great-Gran on Sunday afternoon. I held his hand tightly when we went into the ward. It wasn't the way I'd thought it would be. I wanted it to be very white and neat and tidy with nurses in blue dresses and little frilly caps. It was a big strange messy place with sad people slumped in beds or hunched in wheelchairs. One old man was crying. I nearly cried too.

'Are you sure you're OK, Lizzie?' Sam whispered, bending down to me. 'We can go straight back home if you want.'

I *did* want to go home. But I also wanted to see Great-Gran, though I was very worried she'd look sad and scary now.

'I want to see her,' I said in a teeny-tiny voice.

'OK. She's over here,' said Sam, and he led me to Great-Gran's bed.

Sam's hand was damp. He seemed scared too.

Great-Gran was lying crookedly on the pillow with her hair sticking up and her eyes shut.

'Are you asleep, Gran?' said Sam, bending over her.

Great-Gran's eyes snapped open. They were still bright blue. But they weren't gleaming.

'How are you today, Gran?' said Sam.

Great-Gran made a cross snorty noise. It was obvious she thought it a pretty stupid question.

'I've brought someone to see you,' said Sam. He gave me a gentle tug forward. 'Look, it's little Lizzie.'

Great-Gran looked. Then her eyes clouded and water seeped out. She made more cross snorty sounds. Her nose started running. She tried to move but her arm wouldn't work properly. She wailed and went *gargle-gargle*.

'What is it, Gran?' Sam said helplessly.

'She wants a hankie,' I said. I found Great-Gran's handbag and got a hankie out. 'Here we are. I'll wipe your eyes first. And then your nose. And here's your comb. We'll do your hair, eh? It's OK. I'm good at doing hair. I do Alice's, don't I?'

I mopped and wiped and combed.

'There!'

Great-Gran still looked bothered, her head on one side.

'Do you want to sit up straight?'

Great-Gran nodded.

Sam helped me pull her up and tidy her pillow. Great-Gran lay back, straight in the bed, seeming much more herself. She looked at me. She opened her mouth. She went *gargle-gargle*, then sighed in despair.

'Try again, Gran,' said Sam.

Great-Gran went *gargle-gargle* and then wailed.

'Never mind. Don't upset yourself,' said Sam, patting her little clenched hand.

Great-Gran couldn't stop being upset. She went *gargle-gargle-gargle-gargle*.

'Don't worry. We'll get you talking soon,' said Sam, a tear sliding down his cheek.

'We'll get you talking *now*,' I said, taking Great-Gran's other hand. 'Of course you can talk – if you really want to. Open your mouth!'

Great-Gran opened her mouth. Sam's mouth fell open too.

'Aha! There's your tongue,' I said. 'And your teeth. So use them, please, Great-Gran. NOW!'

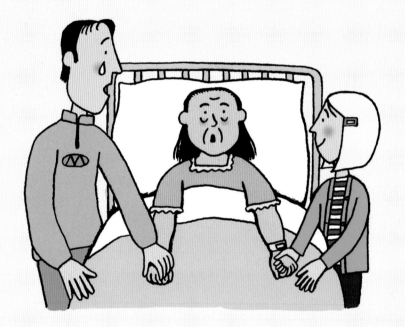

'Cheeky little madam!' said Great-Gran in almost her normal voice.

She sounded cross – but she held on to my hand as if she could never let it go.

☆ CHAPTER EIGHT ☆

Great-Gran didn't die. She didn't get *completely* better. She spent three months learning how to walk again. She had to use a stick and went very, very slowly with a bad limp. One arm wouldn't work properly any more so for a little while she had to have her food cut up. I did it for her, very neatly. I did her hair too and helped her with her stockings and did her shoes up for her with tidy bows.

   Great-Gran didn't need any further help with talking though! For the first few days in hospital she got her words jumbled up and didn't always make sense but by the time she was ready to come home she talked perfectly. She talked too much, telling the doctors and nurses what to do. They didn't always like it. Great-Gran didn't care. Sometimes she got very cross indeed and told them just what she thought of them.

'Can't you keep your grandmother under control?' one nurse said to Sam.

Sam rolled his eyes in a funny way to show this was completely impossible. He tried asking Great-Gran not to be so rude. Great-Gran was very rude indeed to Sam.

I couldn't help getting the giggles.

'I think you should try to be Great-Granny Zipmouth!' I said.

Sam and Mum and Rory and Jake and the nurse all gasped. But Great-Gran didn't get cross with me.

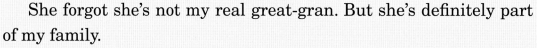

'You're a sparky girl, little Lizzie,' she said. 'You take after me.'

She forgot she's not my real great-gran. But she's definitely part of my family.

She still tells me off sometimes though, now she's back in her flat. I don't really mind. It's because she gets tired out now as one of her legs doesn't work properly. She doesn't like walking very, very

slowly with a limp. But she can go very, very fast when she's outside because she now has an electric scooter to get her to the shops and back. Rory and Jake think Great-Gran's scooter is seriously cool. They keep begging Great-Gran to let them drive it but she won't hear of it.

But guess what! When Sam takes me round to Great-Gran's after school, Great-Gran and I sometimes go on secret trips down to the antique centre to see if there are any more dolls Great-Gran wants to buy. Sometimes I skip along beside Great-Gran. Sometimes I get to sit right on her lap and drive too!

We bought a beautiful big china doll the other day. She's got a pink dress and a white pinafore with tiny pink embroidered roses on it. We gave her a tea party with Alice and Sophie and Charlotte and Edward and Clementine when we got her home.

'But she's not going to live in the trunk with them,' said Great-Gran. 'We'll have to get your dad to build her a special shelf.'

My dad? Then I realized she meant Sam.

'He's good at making shelves,' I said. 'He's made special little shelves for all my mum's CDs.'

Great-Gran snorted. She still isn't all that keen on my mum. Mum isn't all that keen on Great-Gran, come to that. It doesn't matter. I can like them both. And Rory. And Jake. And even Sam. Sometimes.

They all like me too. Especially Great-Gran.

'What are we going to call the new doll, Great-Gran? I've got a good name for her! Rosebud.'

'No, I've chosen her name already. I'm naming her after someone very special,' said Great-Gran.

'Who? *Who?*'

'You sound like an owl! Don't shout! Dear, dear, first you creep around and we can't get a squeak out of you – and now you start shouting at the top of your voice. Calm down. I'm going to call the doll Elizabeth.'

'Elizabeth,' I said. 'Hey, that's *my* name, even though everyone calls me Lizzie!'

'Well, I never,' said Great-Gran and her blue eyes gleamed.

I gave her a great big grin, my mouth *totally* unzipped.

☆ ABOUT THE AUTHOR ☆

JACQUELINE WILSON is one of Britain's bestselling authors, with more than 35 million books sold in the UK alone. She has been honoured with many prizes for her work, including the Guardian Children's Fiction Award and the Children's Book of the Year. Jacqueline is a former Children's Laureate, a professor of children's literature, and in 2008 she was appointed a Dame for services to children's literacy.

Visit Jacqueline's fantastic website at
www.jacquelinewilson.co.uk